FIND YOUR PORPOISE

Also by M. C. Ross

A Dog's Porpoise
Game Over
Nugly

FIND YOUR PORPOISE

M. C. ROSS

Scholastic Inc.

Copyright © 2024 by M. C. Ross

ISBN 978-1-339-01983-3

10 9 8 7 6 5 4 3 2 1   24 25 26 27 28

Printed in the U.S.A.   40
First printing 2024

Book design by Maithili Joshi

For Liffey, again, for taking such good care
of me, and for Dad, again, for taking
such good care of Liffey.

CHAPTER ONE
Lars

"Ruff!"

Lars considered himself a good dog. A great dog, even, if he was being honest. Which he usually was. On account of being so good.

But some things just had to be said. Things that justified being forceful with your tone. Possibly even a bit...rough.

"Ruff! Wroof, wroof—RUFF!"

"Coming through! Sorry, excuse me! Excuse us! Coming through!"

Right, Lars thought. *That's what I just said.*

But he'd take all the help he could get. This was an all-paws-on-deck situation. Ogunquit, Maine, was a great town for many things: Beautiful ocean views, delicious seafood, and kind tourists who were willing to slip certain dogs seafood, even when certain human adults said, *"Please* don't give him more seafood—you can't *imagine* the smell."

But Ogunquit, with its narrow and wandering streets, was *not* a great place to find wide sidewalks. Which was a problem, as Lars was currently barreling down one of those sidewalks at remarkable speed, with his adopted human, Natalie Prater, hot on his heels.

Every corner brought new obstacles. Pedestrians emerged from shops and leaped aside in shock. A seagull investigating a dropped lobster roll squawked at Lars's approach, then exploded into flight. And almost overnight, the town had become covered in a layer of fall's final leaves, scattered across the ground like colorful slip risks, which Lars thoughtfully cleared away for Natalie as they ran.

That was how it worked: Lars was the advance guard and Natalie was public relations. This was good, because there was a record number of tourists on the streets for this late in the season, the reason for which had nothing to do with all those beautiful leaves and everything to do with Natalie and Lars.

"Out of the way, please! Sorry! Thank you!"

"Wroof!"

They made a good team, and as a result, they made good time. And that was crucial, because today was their first day at their new job.

That job was on a boat.

And that boat could *not* be allowed to leave the harbor without them on it.

This was why they ran. This was also why Natalie was dressed like, well, someone who was about to go work on a boat in Maine in late October. Her usual running shoes had been swapped out for deck boots, insulated with bright-orange woolly socks. The socks matched a wool sweater and hat, accompanied by a puffy reflective shell jacket, and all this was layered over a shining black wet suit. It was far from an ideal running outfit, but here Natalie was, keeping up with Lars at full speed, and still managing to get enough air in her lungs to apologize loudly to people as they passed. Lars's heart swelled with love and pride, as it tended to happen when he was around Natalie. One of Lars's favorite things about his adopted human was how determined she could be when she set her mind on something. This was a girl who could not be slowed down by heavy clothes or unusually crowded sidewalks. Perhaps the only thing that could have slowed her down was the law itself. And even the law wouldn't dare to—

"Natalie Prater, slow down!" called the mayor of Ogunquit.

Well, never mind.

Even as the wind rushed through Lars's ears, causing them to flop and bounce, his keen canine hearing could still detect the slight hitch of Natalie's breath behind him. Clearly she didn't love the thought of upsetting Mayor Maher, who had just come out of the Coveside Café a few dozen yards ahead of them, somehow managing to blow on his coffee and frown at the same time. Ogunquit was the kind of small, tight-knit community where everyone knew your name—even the mayor. Most of the time this was great, except when you were trying to get away with something. Then it felt more like living in a town full of hall monitors, some of whom had the power to send you to prison. Not that Mayor Maher *would*. But, you know. He *could*.

For a moment, Lars worried that Natalie might actually stop running. Then:

"Natalie Prater, speed up!" yelled Nancy Jane, one of the friendliest people in Ogunquit—and Natalie's and Lars's next-door neighbor. She had strolled out of the café right after the mayor, and now she gave them both a big friendly wave. "You're almost there! You too, Lars!"

And sure enough, Natalie's hitched breath became a

joyful laugh, and her footfalls got even faster. Lars barked with joy himself and picked up his pace to match. Within seconds, they were racing past Nancy Jane, who grinned mischievously at them both as she reached out her hand and wrapped it around Mayor Maher's. For his part, the mayor said nothing; he just blushed furiously, which was typical. Everyone in town knew that even though the two adults had known each other for forty years, Nancy Jane had the everlasting ability to fluster the mayor with just about anything she said.

Nancy Jane was also right: Lars and Natalie *were* almost there. The Coveside Café was not called that for nothing; passing it meant that they had reached the end of Shore Road, Ogunquit's unofficial main street, and entered the mouth of Perkins Cove, the small inlet harboring Ogunquit's fleet of boats, from fishing and lobster boats to dories, dinghies, and even docked pleasure yachts.

Lars was no stranger to the cove, and this was his favorite part of the approach. Here, buildings and beech trees gave way to reveal the gleam of the ocean. And while there was nowhere you could go in Ogunquit that did not smell of salt air, it was at this precise turn that the deep cool rush of the Atlantic crashed over Lars's nose. The brine, the boat wax, the slight tang of seaweed—it was all sensory heaven for a dog like Lars.

It was also probably why he didn't notice the stroller.

"Look out!" Natalie yelled. Presumably she was not trying to warn Lars, but rather Mrs. Reardon, the Secretary and Treasurer of the Ogunquit Lobstermen's Union and, currently, innocent mother pushing her infant daughter directly into Lars's path. But Lars, always eager to please, took the warning, anyway. In a move he hadn't had to perform for years, Lars flung himself forward and down, his front and back legs stretched out until he was nearly one long horizontal stripe of dog. He slid under the slim space between the stroller and the pavement, popping back up on the other side with a snort, a wag, and no discernible reduction in speed.

Mrs. Reardon cried out in astonishment, while Cassie Reardon clapped and giggled from her stroller throne. Natalie just waved apologetically as they ran past the Reardons.

"See you at the dock!" she said.

And Lars couldn't hide a doggy grin, his tongue flopping out the side of his mouth as they continued to run.

He'd lived on his own for years before he found Natalie and her family, and even though he'd grown used to a life with fewer daring evasive maneuvers, an old stray dog could still bust out a few good tricks.

Right now, though, the only trick Lars needed to execute was a sharp right turn. At last, after pounding past the antique store, the souvenir shop, and Barnacle Barry's Seafood and Restaurant, they had reached the heart of Perkins Cove, and with it, the dock. Natalie's deck boots thudded on the wooden boards as they descended toward the water, when a cry rang out:

"Hey!"

Okay. *That* was one voice they would never dare ignore. With varying levels of success, perhaps due to varying levels of legs, Natalie and Lars both attempted to halt their own wild momentum, leading to a brief moment of skidding on the wet planks of the dock before ultimately ending up in front of one very bemused, very tanned man.

"Hi, Dad," Natalie said, as Lars fell into what he hoped was a respectful sitting position beside her.

Jim Prater was a good fisherman and, in Lars's opinion, an even better dad. But if there was one big flaw in his parenting armor (other than his absurdly strict opinions on the recommended daily amount of bacon-wrapped scallops for dogs), it was this: He often looked stern without really trying to. Then, when a time came that he really *did* want to look stern, he just couldn't quite manage it. Like now, as he unsuccessfully tried to hide his laughter while gazing down at the sheepish, panting pair in front of him.

"That's some unsafe dock behavior you were just modeling for the tourists, huh?" Mr. Prater said. "I don't remember hearing about that as one of your new job duties."

"Job?" said the man standing just behind Mr. Prater, whose conversation Natalie and Lars had clearly interrupted. "What job?"

"Sorry, Dad. We didn't want to be late. Hi, Mr. Rosenberg," Natalie said, nodding to Barry Rosenberg—Barnacle Barry himself, owner of Barnacle Barry's Seafood and Restaurant, and frequent employer of Mr. Prater, whose fishing boat, *The Marina*, provided said seafood to said restaurant.

Mr. Prater was sliding back the sleeve of his own shell jacket to look at a beaten-up waterproof watch. "You guys have plenty of time," he pointed out.

"We do *now*," Natalie conceded. It was hard to tell if

she was blushing or just flushed from running in the October air. "But we woke up late."

"We" feels like a strong word choice, Lars thought. After all, he was the one who had sat barking outside Natalie's bedroom door this morning until she had stumbled out, rubbing at her eyes with stretched-out pajama sleeves, her dirty-blonde hair stuck out at angles Lars had previously only seen in certain clumps of kelp. And he was pretty sure he'd heard her walk directly into the door before opening it.

To be honest, this kind of thing had been happening more and more recently. While it was true that Natalie was unstoppable once she'd built up a head of steam, in the months since she'd turned thirteen, it had seemingly become harder and harder for her to get... sufficiently steamed. In her defense—and Lars was always ready to come to Natalie's defense—the girl was busy. On top of getting ready for this new job, the start of eighth grade had brought a slew of new commitments, from homework to Natalie joining the swim team.

It could be hard to balance work, school, family, and friends, especially when you suddenly found yourself with more friends than ever before. *And* more family;

last year, Maria Prater—Natalie's mother and Mr. Prater's ex-wife—had remarried and become Maria Dugnutt, officially making Natalie the stepdaughter of one Bob Dugnutt, also known as Diver Bob, the town goofball who gave aquatic animal sightseeing tours for kids and tourists. Over the past year and a half, Lars had watched Natalie make an effort to grow closer to Diver Bob, but there was still some oddness to the relationship—partly just because Diver Bob was, given his whole deal, kind of an odd guy. But partly because all those late-in-the-season tourists were here for one thing, and that thing was...

Well... it was complicated. Enough to make any girl want to sleep in more. And Lars understood that—really, he did. But at a time when he was already seeing much less of Natalie than he would have liked (he had yet to convince any relevant authority that he should be allowed to attend school with her), Lars couldn't help but flash back to the loneliness of his stray years and worry: If Natalie had so much trouble this morning making time for the new job she was so excited for... what if, someday soon, she had trouble making time for *Lars*?

Just then, Natalie's hand found the perfect spot

behind Lars's ears, the spot she loved to pet when she was anxious about something and wanted to be reminded that Lars was by her side. Conveniently, Natalie's favorite way to make herself feel better also made *Lars* feel better. His tail swept across the dock and his head rose to meet her hand, all worries forgotten for the moment.

Mr. Prater apparently knew his daughter well enough to notice her nervousness, too, because he uncrossed his arms and bent down to give Lars a comforting scritch. This was shaping up to be a banner morning for Lars, who considered Mr. Prater's scritches to be especially valuable (his hands always smelled like fish).

"Well, you're here now," Mr. Prater said. "You excited about your first day on the job?"

Natalie nodded enthusiastically.

"I was studying for it all night," she said.

"Okay, again, what is this about a job?" Barnacle Barry asked. "Is she officially on our staff now? Should I be adding her to payroll?" He paused, seemingly experiencing a minor implosion somewhere deep inside: "Is the *dog* on my payroll?"

"Not today, Mr. Rosenberg." Natalie laughed.

"Yeah," Mr. Prater huffed in fake offense. "She found someone who'll pay her better than I would."

For someone standing on a dock in a quiet cove, Mr. Rosenberg was doing a great job of looking completely at sea.

"But you love helping on your dad's boat," he said to Natalie. "If *that* isn't the big new job you're so excited about, then what could it possibly—"

BEEEEP!

An absolutely ridiculous noise, loud and squeaky, as if a clown nose had been squeezed into a megaphone, echoed across the harbor.

"All aboard Diver Bob's Sea Life Tours: *Winter Edition!*" blared a voice from the end of the dock. "Last call for all sailors! *That means* you, *Natalie and Lars Prater!*"

Lars hopped back up on his feet, and Natalie laughed.

"*That's* my new job," Natalie said. "Now if you'll excuse us—I'd *really* rather not be late to my first day working for my stepdad. Good luck fishing today, Dad!"

Suddenly Natalie was running again, making her way for the farthest end of the dock, where a big colorful boat was waiting for her. She'd taken off so quickly that even Lars was surprised, and as he whirled away from Mr. Prater to chase her, Lars felt happily foolish for ever having worried about Natalie, who was clearly adjusting just fine to this new chapter of her life, and who didn't seem even slightly tired.

As Lars turned up the gangway and followed Natalie onto Diver Bob's boat, he searched for a way to express that happiness. In the end, there was just one thing that had to be said:

"Ruff!"

CHAPTER TWO
Natalie

Natalie was incredibly nervous about this new chapter of her life. She was also extremely tired.

But she was *also* on a boat.

So basically, everything was fine.

And getting better by the second. Just moments ago, Diver Bob's ship—the *Searchin' Urchin*—had passed between the raised arms of the drawbridge marking the border between Perkins Cove and the wider Atlantic. White caps of foam leaped up to wave hello in the flickering spaces between rocks and hillocks; then the *Urchin* sailed out of the mouth of the cove and onto the open ocean.

Natalie took a deep breath and smiled a genuine, bright smile. Salt, wind, and water crashed and clashed around her, blasting the sleep out of her eyes. It had been like this as long as she could remember, ever since she'd giggled through her first full day out on her father's fishing boat, back when she'd sat in her mom's lap because she was smaller than some of the fish in the nets. Of course, that was before her mom had moved out. But even after that, in the wake of her parents' divorce, being out on the water was what had brought peace and happiness back into Natalie's life, like a tide returning to shore. For as long as Natalie could remember, the ocean had been just as much her next-door neighbor as Nancy Jane, and just like Nancy Jane, it always knew how to make her feel better.

Which was good because Natalie didn't have time to be anything other than her best.

"Alright!" she said, clapping her hands. "Who's ready for a *safety demonstration?*"

About thirty pairs of eyes stared up at her. Many of the eyes belonged to small children. Those eyes stared *way* up at her. The only sounds were the motor and the waves.

"A safety demonstration featuring...my friend *Lars?*"

At the sound of his name, Lars hopped up onto a fishy-smelling cooler next to Natalie, and a boatload of children broke into yelling and cheers.

As Natalie passed out name tags and used Lars to model proper life-jacket usage, she was more grateful than ever for the cold sea air keeping her awake and alert. She'd told her father the truth when she said she'd spent last night studying for her new job as Diver Bob's "First Mate and Nature-Narrating Lieutenant." (Diver Bob had unusual ideas about the maritime chain of command.)

What she *hadn't* told her father was that she'd been studying for some of that morning, too, staying up and cramming until well after midnight. In part, that was because the material was genuinely interesting. The job required her to know all kinds of facts about aquatic life, and there were few things Natalie loved more than learning exactly that. Did you know that sea scallops have two hundred eyes? Or that baby seals can swim from the moment they're born? Natalie hadn't, but now she did, and she was excited to share what she'd learned with everyone else on this boat.

It's just that it would have been supercool to have learned those things sometime *before* ten o'clock last night. But before ten, she'd had homework. And before homework, she'd had her weekly Friday night dinner with her mom and Diver Bo—with Bob. And before *that*, swim practice, and school, and walking Lars before school, and so on.

Natalie loved having all these things and people in her life (except maybe the homework). But she also loved sleep and having time to just goof around. And lately, both of those resources were in short supply.

Case in point: In the brief moment Natalie had paused to think about this, one of the children had begun to frantically wave their hand up and down.

When she saw who it was, Natalie couldn't help but laugh.

"Yes, Sammy?" she asked, smiling at Sammy Reardon, Mrs. Reardon's oldest child, who wasn't very old at all. He looked ridiculous stuffed into a puffy life jacket over an even puffier parka, but it was nice to see a familiar face on the boat, rather than another hard-to-impress tourist.

"When are we gonna get to see the por—"

"Hold on," Natalie cut in. "Where's your dad? Shouldn't you be accompanied by an adult?"

"Mom said you could accommo...accomplice... accompany me," Sammy informed her. "Since you're my babysitter and all."

Ah, yes. Another part-time job Natalie was currently balancing on top of everything else. She spared a quick glance to the rest of the boat, making sure they weren't getting restless. Upon seeing several rows of passengers all happily taking photos of the ocean (or a proudly posing Lars), Natalie decided she had a moment to kneel next to Sammy.

"Well, that's okay this time…because now you can tell your mom we're even," Natalie whispered. "Lars and I kind of had a run-in with her and your sister on the way over here. Were they dropping you off?"

At the mention of his sister, Sammy frowned.

"Yeah. Cassie can't come on the tour because she's a boring *baby*."

Natalie laughed. "I think Cassie's a *cool* baby," she said. "She likes Lars, for one thing."

Sammy shook his head. He wasn't buying it.

"*I* liked Lars first," he reminded her, in case this would help Natalie realize the one-year-old in question clearly lacked an innovative spirit.

It was funny to watch the normally cheerful Sammy cross his arms and stare out moodily at the ocean, but Natalie couldn't blame him for having big feelings. When you were young and your family dynamic changed, it could be pretty tough to process.

She knew that all too well.

Her gaze followed Sammy's across the water, and

there, a few cable lengths away, was her dad. Well, his boat, at least, sailing out for another day of fishing; she couldn't see him, but she could see the big letters splashed across the side of the vessel, *The Marina*. If you squinted, you could just make out the stripes of new paint covering the name. Once, the boat had been named *The Maria P.* for Maria Prater, Natalie's mother. Then, as a show of goodwill in the wake of her remarriage, Mr. Prater had rechristened the boat *The Maria D.* Afterward, apparently second-guessing whether that gesture might come off as weird, he'd painted over the letter, leaving just: *The Maria*. And then after *that*, he'd completely panicked, and decided to just play it as safe as possible, slapping a new letter in the middle and landing at *The Marina*.

For Natalie, seeing that hurried paint job was just like seeing Sammy's stern expression right now—it was funny, yes, but it came from a place of real worry. How were you supposed to act when your family suddenly got bigger? What behavior was too clingy? What was too distant?

And those fears could be infectious. When Dad had joked that working on the *Urchin* would pay Natalie more than working on *The Marina*...had that been a joke? Or was he expressing some real insecurity? She hoped not; she loved her father and knew he worked hard, and she would have felt terrible if he didn't know that. And anyway, what did he have to worry about? Business had never been better these past few years, ever since they'd all become so well known for—

"Ahoy there, matey!" boomed a voice. They must have gotten far enough out from shore for their first stop, because Diver Bob had cut the engine and come out from the cockpit to join them on the aft deck.

"Are we playing favorites with the deckswabs?" he asked Natalie.

"I would *never*," Natalie said solemnly, aware that some of the passengers had turned to watch this first-ever interaction between their captain and first mate.

"Really? *I* would." Diver Bob shrugged. "For example, you're *my* favorite, hands down."

He turned to the rest of the ship.

"Oops. You didn't all hear that, did you? You're *all* my favorite. Well, all of you who agree with everything I say. So, basically, just Lars. Right, Lars?"

Lars barked, and once again, Natalie had to smile.

Diver Bob was a fundamentally silly man. As his recently teenage stepdaughter, Natalie was faintly aware she should have been annoyed by this, or at least cringed more, as was the way of teenagers everywhere. But actually, the most she'd ever felt that way was a few years ago when the divorce had been rawer. Now, though...

The only thing sillier than a silly man, it turned out, was trying to stay mad at one. Bob Dugnutt was so hopelessly, well-meaningly dorky that it felt sort of like trying to hold a grudge against a banana cream pie. And Natalie *liked* banana cream pie. So really, why bother?

"Speaking of agreeing with everything I say..." Diver Bob mused loudly, stroking his chin. "*I* say it's time for us to see what's in the sea! Who wants to help me drop the anchor?"

Kids clamored to help, and Natalie took this as her cue to get moving. This part, at least, had required no studying; she'd grown up taking these tours, just like any other kid in Ogunquit, and she knew exactly what was supposed to happen now.

While Diver Bob finished with the anchor and began to pull on his drysuit, Natalie hurried to raise a blue-and-white "diver down" flag, signaling any passing ships to slow down and be careful. Then she ran to help Diver Bob collect the things he would need for his dive. That meant the scuba mask and air tank any diver would want, but on the *Searchin' Urchin*, it also meant something else: A custom-built waterproof video camera that, when linked up to the big TV screen at the front of the deck, would allow Diver Bob to livestream all the astounding animals and freaky fish he found on the ocean floor.

As Natalie made sure that the TV was working, Bob waddled his way to the stern, crowded on all sides by children eager to help push him off, like a Pied Piper in flippers. Lars, riled up by the excitement, let out a few celebratory barks, which reminded Natalie to wrap a hand around his collar, making sure he didn't get too close to the edge of the boat. As Natalie knew from experience, Lars was an excellent swimmer, but the trick was to make sure he went into the ocean on *purpose* instead of by *accident*.

If Natalie stretched, she could just manage to press the buttons on the TV with one hand while holding on to Lars with the other. This wasn't too bad. As long as no one needed anything el—

"Natalie?" Diver Bob's voice emerged from behind a pile of giggling kids. "Did you happen to see my hood liner?"

Of course. Natalie felt her cheeks burn as she

abandoned the TV to grab the warm head covering that she'd forgotten to give her stepdad. But no wonder she'd forgotten—Bob didn't normally *wear* a liner under his hood, because he didn't normally run his tours in the middle of the cold New England autumn. In fact, he'd *never* run them at this time. This was his first ever "Winter Edition" tour, and Natalie was already coming close to screwing it up.

Bob, however, either didn't feel this way or simply didn't care, happily accepting the hood from her and pulling it over his curly hair before sealing it under his drysuit.

"Thank you kindly, first matey." He beamed. "Wouldn't want to catch a cold while I catch clams, would I, folks?"

As reactions went, it was much milder than the nightmare scenario Natalie had just played out in her head—something along the lines of "Attention, everyone, my stepdaughter has become so scatterbrained she almost dropped me into fifty-degree water as if it were the warmest day in July." Still, she'd wanted to be perfect for her first day, and it only made her feel guiltier when a young girl in the middle of the throng raised her hand and asked, "Wait, don't you need anything else, though? Won't it be *cold* down there?"

"Oh, it's *very* cold. That's part of why we're here." Diver Bob's eyes gleamed, and Natalie recognized that gleam from years of firsthand experience. It was the gleam that allowed you to overlook all the cheesiness, all the lame jokes, all the *everything* of Bob Dugnutt. Because it was the gleam he gave off whenever he was doing what was clearly his favorite thing in the world: educating kids about the ocean and blowing their minds while doing it.

"See, cold is *good*," Bob explained, the audience spellbound in the face of his pleasantly unhinged grin. "In the ocean, cold is *life*. The colder the water is, the more oxygen it can hold. We have a saying on this boat. 'More makes more, and more makes merry.' Oxygen feeds algae. Algae feed shrimp and tiny little fishes. And shrimp and tiny little fishes feed..." Suddenly his arms were outstretched, and his voice was an enormous roar. "*Big, hungry* fishes!"

Kids fell back around him like hysterical bowling pins, and even the parents on the benches cracked a smile.

Well, most of them. One—a man with light brown hair and glasses, whose name tag read ADAM in all caps— maintained an inquisitive, almost impatient expression.

Natalie hadn't seen him around before, which in a town as small as Ogunquit meant he was either new or a tourist.

"But that's only *part* of why we're here, right?" Adam asked suddenly, his voice cutting through the laughter. "I mean, you've never taken passengers out this late in the year before. What would you say is the *real* reason this is happening right now?"

His tone was oddly intense, and Natalie craned her neck, trying to see just whose parent he was. But with all the kids crowded around Diver Bob, there was no real way to know who belonged to whom.

"Great point," Bob admitted, his good cheer unfaltering even in the face of this interrogation. "Most years, this is the weekend I start my winter job, diving for scallops. So don't worry"—here, he winked at the girl who had first asked him about the temperature— "I'm plenty used to the cold. But as for why I've taken you all with me today"—and here, he turned to Natalie, and everyone else shifted to follow his gaze— "Lieutenant First Mate Natalie can explain that for you. Can't you, Natalie?"

Theoretically, well…she could. In fact, Natalie knew precisely the reason they were all out here today.

In many ways, she herself *was* that reason. But the story behind it was so outlandish, so unbelievable, that Natalie hardly knew where to begin. And while normally she had no fear of public speaking (Ogunquit's monthly town hall meetings quickly taught you to either speak up or miss out), she wasn't so sure she had her stepdad's gift for keeping things light and goofy.

And there was something about the way Adam was glaring at her—like she'd done something wrong without even knowing it—that was decidedly neither light nor goofy. *Had* she done something wrong? It was like he knew what she was about to say, and he already didn't like it. For a moment, it all felt like more than Natalie could handle.

Then she tore herself away from Adam's eyes and found Lars looking up at her. In sharp contrast to Adam, Lars's eyes were filled with love and pride, as if Natalie had already done everything *right* without even trying. And when she looked up at Bob's face, she found he was looking at her in much the same way.

More than Natalie could handle? No way. *More makes merry*, Bob had said. And remembering the face he'd made while saying it, Natalie flashed a merry grin of her own.

"It's kind of a long story," she said. "I have this friend. Or I guess ... *these* frien—"

Suddenly she was interrupted by a familiar sound from beyond the edge of the boat:

Puff!

And Natalie's grin grew that much wider.

"Actually, how about you all just see for yourself?" she said. "Here they are now!"

And as kids and adults alike raced to the side of the boat to get a better look, the real reason for their voyage made itself clear.

It was a reason that had first started appearing off the shores of Ogunquit a year and a half ago, noticed first by Natalie and Lars one incredible day out on the water, and then swiftly noticed by many, many other people.

It was the reason tourists now lined the streets of Ogunquit long after tourist season was meant to have ended.

It was the reason Diver Bob tours were now selling out well into the winter.

And it was, at least partially, the reason Lars and Natalie were Diver Bob's newest, most valuable employees.

Now, that reason—actually, one of several—arced out of the ocean, shooting water out of its spout as it did so, leaving a vapor trail that glittered in the autumn sunlight before rejoining the waves below.

The reasons were porpoises.

First one, then two, then more—a whole family, or *pod*, of harbor porpoises, surfacing and spinning in the water in front of the *Urchin*.

They were here to see their friends.

They were here to see Natalie and Lars.

And of all the new friends Natalie had made this year, she couldn't help but smile and think that these were the friends who proved it best of all: More most *definitely* made merry.

CHAPTER THREE
Bangor

To understand how a pod of harbor porpoises had become friends with a stray dog and a human girl, you had to understand something about Bangor.

Bangor was a harbor porpoise with a problem.

Most harbor porpoise problems are very simple. Either you want to eat something or something wants to eat you. In both cases, the solution is more or less the same: *swim away.*

This was also the case for other, less life-or-death porpoise problems. A boat being too noisy? A human getting too close for comfort? The same answer worked for both: *just swim away.* It was the simple one-step program of harbor porpoises everywhere. After all, most of them were shy, reclusive creatures. Even though they lived close to shorelines where humans could see them quite often, the vast majority of harbor porpoises ultimately preferred playing with their own kind.

Bangor's problem, though, was this: Bangor liked playing with *everyone*.

It wasn't the kind of problem you could swim away from. And even if you could, Bangor most likely wouldn't have done so. This was due to another fact about Bangor and, depending on who you asked, an even bigger problem: Bangor pretty much always wanted to swim *toward*.

For example:

Puff!

Kids cried out and parents gasped as Bangor made his closest appearance yet, breaching for a breath just a few feet away from the funny loud man's funny loud boat. Bangor hardly knew what felt better, the adulation or the air rushing over his smooth dorsal fin as he curved back down into the water, rejoicing in a rush of bubbles before bending back up and starting the whole thing all over again.

Technically this wasn't showing off. Harbor porpoises, after all, were known to surface for air as often as four times every minute. Could Bangor help it if the crowd went wild every time he appeared? No, he could not. It was as natural as, well, breathing.

That said, could he perhaps help the fact that each

time the humans cheered, he indulged in a swell of joy that practically lifted him—actually, that very much *did* lift him—back out of the water, in search of even more praise and applause?

Well, maybe he could have helped *that*. Certain members of his pod certainly thought so. Which was, in the end, part of why Bangor had a problem.

But other members of the pod had other thoughts entirely.

"Eee-eee-ee-e!"

A small streak of gray shot past Bangor, releasing a classic harbor porpoise hello—a clicking sound that started off low and then swiftly swept higher in speed and pitch. Based on both size and sheer friendliness, that had to be Bristol, Bangor's little sister. As the baby of the family, she had not quite figured out that the humans could not always hear or understand her attempts to greet them. But she sure loved to try, and Bangor loved her for that.

Why don't they click back? Bristol squeaked curiously. *Do you think they misheard me?*

Hmm. I don't know. It was a harbor porpoise's natural state of being to smile, so Bangor wasn't even trying to hide his amusement as he bumped against his sister

31

encouragingly. *Maybe you should try a jump to let them know you're here.*

Great idea! As always, Bristol was eager to prove herself to her older brother, and in seconds she had shot up out of the sea, earning another round of oohs and aahs from the spectators above. This clearly thrilled Bristol as she shot back down around Bangor and burned off her excitement in tight, zooming circles.

Just then, a cacophony of clicks came from behind them, like a challenge:

That's nothing. Watch this!

And in a blur of movement, something flashed above them. The shape was so large that it temporarily blocked out the sun—and so fast that it passed in milliseconds, leaving a corona of bright light in its wake as it burst beyond the water, propelled by its own momentum into the air, soaring in a way harbor porpoises hardly ever did. The only thing louder than the surprise of the humans was the splash as the newcomer fell back into the water.

Great job, Belfast! Bristol cried.

Great job, Belfast, Bangor chimed in bemusedly.

Belfast was their big brother, with an emphasis on *big*, and a further emphasis on *bold*, *brash*, and *bet I can outswim you—let's race!*

But there would be no races today—at least not yet. Because here came their mother, Kittery, circling around the pod protectively and clicking a warning: *Careful. Don't get too close.*

Kittery was a much more old-fashioned harbor porpoise than any of her kids, and she tended to keep her distance around humans, even proven friendly ones like Natalie Prater.

It's totally safe, Mom! Chirped Bristol. *The boat's not even running!*

There are still humans on that boat, Kittery reminded them. Bangor noticed that she hadn't surfaced yet—a porpoise could hold its breath for over six minutes if it wanted to, and Kittery clearly wanted to. *And humans are wild animals. Back me up, York ... York?*

A portly porpoise swam slowly into view—well, slowly for a harbor porpoise. To the surprise of nobody, Uncle York was bringing up the rear as the final member of the pod, hanging back in case there were any extra fish they'd missed on their approach to the boat.

However, and *very* much to the surprise of Kittery, Uncle York continued past all of them toward the boat.

Hold that thought, York clicked.

And then he didn't just come up for air but stuck his

whole snout out of the water and kept it there, bucking and clicking until a flash of silver arced across the surface of the sea and slid right into York's waiting jaws.

Splash! York fell back down into the water and swam smugly around the pod.

Humans are *wild*, he marveled to the ocean at large. *They just* give *you their fish. For* free*! I'll never get over it! Your friends are great, Bangor.*

Right, so.

How *did* Bangor meet his human friends?

Just a year and a half ago, Bangor had been living like any other harbor porpoise, swimming and playing with his pod up in the northern Gulf of Maine. But though he may have *lived* like them, Bangor didn't *feel* like them. While Kittery and the others were content with the life that they had, Bangor had always wanted more—more adventures and more friends to play with. He would dart along the edges of coastal shelves and slip round the shipping routes of boats, wondering where they were headed, and if he ever might go there, too.

Then one night, adventure came calling for Bangor.

The call sounded like rain.

The pod had been heading home from a successful

fish hunt when the waves above them had started to ripple. Then they started to roar. It was a storm, massive and pounding, and it turned the ocean into a noisy nightmare. For a pod of harbor porpoises, who relied on echolocation to both see and talk, it was like being trapped in total darkness. Bangor had swum as fast as he could, frantic to get his bearings, but the maelstrom refused to let up. It wasn't until after a full night of moving south along the coast that Bangor finally lost the storm. Unfortunately, he also lost his pod in the process.

Maybe he would have turned around and found them. Maybe he would have decided that adventures were overrated and being alone was scary. But before he could do that, Bangor saw that he *wasn't* alone. There, just ahead of him was the strangest thing he'd ever seen in his life: four scruffy legs, thrashing about in the water like a fuzzy turtle who'd forgotten how to swim.

As it would turn out, Natalie and Lars had gotten caught in the same storm as Bangor and his pod. They had been out on Natalie's father's boat, apparently helping him with his own fish hunt, when the storm had taken them by surprise—and thrown Lars overboard in a big wave.

Bangor wouldn't find this out until much later, well after he'd first spotted Lars and thought, *Are fur turtles . . . a thing? And if so, are they* supposed *to flail around like that?* All he knew in that moment was that he loved making new friends—and that new friends were much harder to make if they weren't alive.

Bangor made a snap decision. Within seconds, a stunned Lars found himself rising out of the water—and riding on the back of a harbor porpoise, who deposited him back on the solid shores of Perkins Cove. The Praters caught up to them shortly thereafter, and upon discovering her dog safe, sound, and playing in the water with a miraculously appearing harbor porpoise, Natalie had splashed right in as well, overwhelmed with gratitude—and an unbreakable bond between friends had been born.

At least, Bangor had hoped it was unbreakable. After a spring spent swimming around Perkins Cove, summer had rolled around, bringing with it a spike in the water temperature, one too warm for harbor porpoises to handle. Bangor had been forced to return north, where he found his family, all overjoyed to see him again—as he was overjoyed to see them. But all summer long, he'd thought about how much fun he'd had with his new friends down south, and wondered if they still thought of him, as well. When the days grew shorter and the water began to cool again, he'd convinced his family to come back down along the coast and meet the people who had taken such good care of their prodigal porpoise.

You'll love them, he'd chirped incessantly to his mother. *They helped feed me and kept me safe. And they have this toy called a tennis ball—it's* amazing.

Can you eat it? That was Uncle York, floating by upside down. He'd been known to drift wherever the ocean currents rolled him, even if they rolled him onto his back.

Bangor considered this. *I suppose you* can. *I'm not sure if you* should.

York snorted a bubble out of his blowhole. *I'd like to be the judge of* that.

And I'd *like to be the judge of these humans,* Kittery weighed in at last. She'd been swimming alongside her son in contemplative silence, but after several hours (okay, days) (okay, months) of pleading from Bangor, she seemed to be coming around. *I only want what's best for my family. And if what you're telling me is true...perhaps this is it.*

That had been last October. Upon making the return

trip, news of not one but *five* harbor porpoises in Perkins Cove had traveled fast, and within an hour of their arrival, Natalie and Lars had come running to the beach to greet Bangor and his pod as old friends. As for the rest of Ogunquit, they treated the pod more like beloved local celebrities.

This both helped and did not help Bangor's argument with Kittery.

On the one fluke, playing and eating were a harbor porpoise's two favorite pastimes, and the humans down here were more than happy to supply both, always up for a swim or to toss their new friends some fish.

On the other fluke, Perkins Cove, which had already been a busy boat harbor to begin with, was now also full of tourists and flashing cameras, eager to spot the famously friendly harbor porpoises, and Bangor could tell that Kittery found all the attention a bit overwhelming. He was pretty sure his siblings did, too, sometimes, even if they kept it hidden—Bristol because she wanted to impress her older brothers, and Belfast because he wanted to seem like the cool older brother who deserved to be impressed. Only Uncle York, blessed with a one-current mind, seemed as completely at peace in Ogunquit as he was way up north.

In the end, Kittery proved as perceptive a mother as she was a careful one. She could see the joy her family had found here in the southern gulf, and after a long summer away, she had given her blessing to make another triumphant return.

Which had brought Bangor here. For the past few weeks, the pod had been seen all up and down the coast of Ogunquit, puffing and piercing through cold cresting waves, eliciting cries of elation everywhere they appeared. But wherever he went, Bangor always listened hard for one cry in particular—well, more of a bark. That was the sound that had started his new life. It was the sound that meant his best friend was near.

And it was the sound that had just echoed across the water from the *Searchin' Urchin,* as a flying brown blur went leaping off the edge of the boat, followed swiftly by a human girl.

To Bangor's delight—matched only, perhaps, by the delight of the onlookers on the *Urchin*—Natalie and Lars had dropped in to say hello.

Phones were whipped out and mutters of astonishment were heard as the porpoises swam up around their friends. Lars found himself doggy paddling happily between Bangor and Bristol. His swimming skills,

Bangor noticed, had come a long way since the day Lars had first tipped off of Mr. Prater's boat. Of course, he was still slower than even York on one of his slowest days—but Bangor loved the funny way his tail swished back and forth in the water, and even more than that, he loved seeing his little sister circle excitedly around his best friend.

As Bangor was watching this, he felt a cool hand press gently against his melon, the curving slope of his forehead that allowed him to echolocate better. He rolled his eye up and found Natalie rubbing his head soothingly the way she somehow always knew to do, and leaning in to whisper softly in his highly sensitive ears, "I'm so glad you guys showed up. I was having kind of a stressful day... but you guys just made it all better."

Do you *know what she's saying?* Belfast puffed from a few yards away.

Technically Bangor did not. Human language was clumsy and cluttered with sound, a far cry from the clean crisp clicks and squeaks of porpoise speech. But after spending enough time with them, Bangor had learned to understand a lot about humans from their tone. So it was with both confidence and accuracy that he reported, *She's happy to see us.*

And the feeling was mutual.

For the next fifteen minutes, girl, dog, and pod swam and splashed together. Then, because dogs simply couldn't swim as long as porpoises, Natalie helped Lars back up onto the *Urchin* and worked him over with a warm, fluffy towel, while the porpoises got a new human visitor in exchange. Diver Bob, all sealed up in his drysuit and toting some bizarre piece of human equipment, plunged into the water and, with the help of a bulky weighted belt, descended to the ocean floor. There, his well-rehearsed routine of finding scallops and sculpins was only enhanced by the effect of five curious but respectful porpoises dipping in and out of frame, wondering what was going on, and how or if they were supposed to help.

From far up above the surface came a sound Bangor knew well, amplified by some kind of human technology: Natalie's voice. From the way her pitch rose or fell every time Bob caught a sea cucumber or encountered a cusk, Bangor had come to believe that Natalie was somehow narrating what was happening below them, presumably with the aid of whatever it was Bob kept pointing around in the water. He found it all fascinating, and even though they'd seen this happen before,

Bangor was still a little disappointed when Bob went back to the boat and began pulling up the anchor, signaling the start of the *Urchin*'s return trip to shore.

Can we follow them, Mom? Bangor clicked.

Yeah! Can we? Bristol zigzagged hopefully. *I haven't been to the cove for days, and swimming alongside the boats is so fun!*

Well . . . Kittery wavered.

Last one there's a rotten cod! And with that, Belfast was off. Bangor turned to look at his mother, who just sent up a snort of loving exasperation and took off after her eldest son, signaling for the rest of the pod to do the same.

Bristol was right—swimming alongside boats *was* fun, and with the entire pod escorting the *Urchin* in leaps and puffs, sunshine sliding along their sleek flanks, they made for a remarkable sight.

The closer they got to shore, though, the more nervous Kittery clearly became. Not without reason, either: Perkins Cove was the center for Ogunquit's commercial boating. And while all the boatmen of Ogunquit had very thoughtfully adjusted to their new porpoise neighbors, many of them equipping their boats with alarms called pingers that helped avoid run-ins with the pod, there was no denying that so many noisy boats crowding into one place could make one feel awfully ... crowded.

Alright, kids, Kittery clicked, as the mouth of Perkins Cove appeared before them, dotted with trawlers and skiffs. *I think it's about time to turn around.*

But Bangor, who had just seen Mr. Prater's boat pulling in ahead of them, felt tempted to push his luck. *Come on, Mom!* he urged. *I wanna say hi to Natalie's dad!*

Kittery seemed unmoved. *There are too many humans here. And I'm sure Uncle York is too tired to—York?!*

York had just overtaken Belfast to become the closest one to the *Urchin*.

They have fish, he clicked back to Kittery, in the same blunt and self-explanatory tone one might have used to say, *Well, I've been tied to the boat with a rope, so.*

See? He loves it! Bangor put on a little more speed, trying to give his mom less time to say no. *It's fine!*

Listen, I've been very *patient with all of this.* Kittery's tone was stern enough to shock them all. Even Belfast paused briefly to turn and look back at the matriarch of the pod. *But it is my responsibility to keep you all safe. So much goes on here, we don't know what might happen next—*

And she was right.

Because no one could have anticipated what happened next.

A cry of astonishment went up from one boat. Then another. And then another, like fire leaping across Perkins Cove.

See? Kittery huffed. *Now they've all noticed us, and they'll all be clamoring to—*

Uh, Mom? Bangor clicked. *I don't think they're yelling for us.*

And at that precise moment, a brown flash burst out of the water, moving in a way Bangor had never seen before. Something, or someone, had just introduced themselves to Perkins Cove. Someone who astonished every human they passed. Someone who swam like a lightning bolt who'd decided to try some new moves for a change.

Someone who looked, to Bangor, like a brand-new adventure.

And someone Bangor swam toward.

CHAPTER FOUR
Lars

For the rest of his life, Lars would remember how he had felt at the end of that morning as they pulled back into Perkins Cove. After years of wandering without a true home, wondering if anyone would ever truly love him as their own, Lars's big debut on Diver Bob's boat had felt like the culmination of a life spent longing to belong. And what a culmination it was—from the children lining up for the chance to pet his belly, to his best friend with flippers, Bangor, showing up just to say hi, to (best of all) the way Natalie wrapped him up in that big warm towel afterward, leaned down to kiss his head, and said, "We make a pretty good team, huh?"

That's what he would remember feeling, more than anything else: like he was on a team. Like he was officially a part of the family. He felt lovable and valuable and seen as both these things. He was no longer lost in the literal wilderness, sleeping under bushes or on the edge of scrubby beaches. Finally he had found a safe place as the unquestioned star of his Prater-Dugnutt-porpoise-pod family's eye.

He would remember all this, because the moment he truly felt it—the moment he let himself believe—was the precise moment that *she* appeared, streaking through the water.

She was a river otter.

And somehow, Lars just knew that she would change everything.

In fact, she already had. As shouts rang out around the Cove, the tour-takers once again rushed to the edge of the *Urchin*, with even the grumpy Adam getting up to crane his neck. In an effort to see what all the fuss was about, Natalie got up to join the wall of humans, as well. It all left Lars with just enough time to see a tufty clump of whiskers pop up out of the water before his vision was obscured by blue jeans and L.L. Bean.

But he'd already seen enough. And *smelled*, for that matter, much more than enough.

A river otter.

Oh, Lars knew about river otters. You saw them all over the state, from inland to oceanside, sticking mostly to freshwater streams but happy to zoom up and down the rocky ridges of the coast as well. They thought they were so cute, with their little dark eyes, their big wiggly noses, and their…their little-and-or-big fuzzy brown paws, which they were forever clapping adorably to their mouths. Well, you know what Lars *didn't* think was adorable? *Thumbs!* What kind of nonhuman animal went around having *thumbs?* River otters did, and if you asked him, it was weird. And not for nothing, but river otters *smelled*. They smelled so bad that Lars had even seen *human* noses notice the stench. On a good day, your average river otter smelled like a rotten jumbo shrimp who had decided to wear an old fur coat in the middle of a record-breaking heat wave.

You know. If you asked Lars.

Not that anyone ever did. Humans were obsessed with river otters, as Lars knew all too well. Many was the day, back in his stray life, when he'd been working some dock in Biddeford or Brunswick, *this* close to getting surreptitiously slipped a snack by a trusting ferryman. Then along would come a river otter, popping out of whatever port mouth they'd swum up from before rolling on their back with a *slap* of their long brown tail. And suddenly there went *all* the attention, and Lars's hopes for the day, to boot.

Were they *actually* trying to ruin Lars's day when

they did this? No, he had to admit, they probably were not. In fact, several of them had clearly tried to play with him over the years, bouncing around him in leaps and bounds, squiggling up and down, like some kind of cute and slippery water dog.

It was just that *Lars* liked to think of himself as a cute water dog. He knew it was petty, but there it was: When river otters came around, he'd learned it was his cue to get out of town, because a scruffy, scraggly stray dog was about to seem very unlovable in comparison to a sleek, snuggly-looking otter.

Life's not like that anymore, Lars reminded himself. *You've got a Natalie now.* With whiplash quickness, his whole body rippled as he shook the bad thoughts—and the remaining ocean water—off him, spraying sea salt onto the towel Natalie had draped him in. Well, partially onto the towel; several drops most definitely got on the passengers around him, earning small cries of surprise. A few quickly turned to look at him, including Natalie.

But just as quickly, they all turned back to see where the otter was now.

Including Natalie.

"He's amazing!" Natalie cried, pointing, and through

the gap under her outstretched arm, Lars could only watch as the otter leaped clear out of the water and flew in a rainbow curve of water and refracted light.

"That's a she," said Diver Bob and Adam at the same time, before looking at each other with mutual surprise.

"A fellow fan of marine life, I see!" Diver Bob beamed.

"Something like that." Adam decidedly did not beam back.

"Look!" Natalie had barely noticed any of this, her eyes glued only on the otter. "She's nearing *The Marina*—Oh my gosh, *Dad!*"

Lars jumped up on the cooler for a better view, getting there just in time to see the otter plunge deep beneath the surface of the water. Meanwhile, even across the Cove and over the sound of the astonished crowd, Mr. Prater had heard his daughter's call, and his head snapped straight up to look at her.

This was how Mr. Prater completely missed the river otter bursting into the air behind him, flinging herself over the gunwale, and crashing onto *The Marina*.

The scattered shouts that had been going up from every boat now united in a roar of ecstatic disbelief. To Mr. Prater's credit, he did not look offended or even frightened so much as astonished beyond words by the otter's audacity. Lars could relate.

For a high-noon moment, man and otter stared at each other.

Mr. Prater stepped left, trying to give the otter a clear path to return to the water.

But the otter shimmied to the left, too.

Mr. Prater went right. The otter dodged right.

Mr. Prater widened his legs and raised his hands high in the air, as if to say, "I don't want to do you any harm, or even touch you, but also, notice how big and scary I am."

The otter dashed right through the space between Mr. Prater's legs, catapulted herself atop one of his coolers, stretched out her paws, and—those *thumbs!*—snatched a stray fish that had been left in the netting, popping it right into her mouth. Then, like a slinky that had recently forgotten about gravity, she sprang up off the cooler, over the edge of the boat, and right back into the water.

Flash!

Lars, Natalie, and Adam all turned to look at Diver Bob, who had just taken a photo of the thief in action on his phone.

"Sorry." He grinned sheepishly. "Couldn't resist. But look at this."

He held up the phone screen, and it was, indeed, an irresistible shot. Frozen in a moment of shock, Mr. Prater had dropped his jaw open in an *O* as he watched the otter go over the gunwale with her stolen fish, a sea bass so big that it stuck out both ends of her mouth, making her look like some kind of hastily assembled hammerhead shark. And there, framed right behind the otter, who had somehow positioned herself perfectly between the *R* and the *I*, was the big painted name...

"*Marina*," Natalie breathed.

"Kind of a perfect name for her, no?" Bob's smile had enough wattage to power a small motorboat. "It's like she's announcing herself."

Natalie smiled, too—and then, remembering that the person in the photo was here in real life as well, looked up across the water.

"Dad! Are you okay?!"

"I'm all good!" It took a lot to flap the unflappable Mr. Prater, and he flashed them a double thumps-up from the edge of his boat. But even though he acted calm on the outside, Lars could see he was slowly swiveling his head back and forth, just in case the fish thief returned to the scene of the crime. For now, though, the otter had disappeared beneath the blue, presumably finding a secret spot to enjoy her stolen goods in peace.

"I got the whole thing on camera!" Diver Bob yelled, waving his phone. "This is gonna be great for business!"

"Yours or mine?" Mr. Prater called back.

"Both!"

"Her name is Marina!" That was Sammy Reardon, cupping his hands around his mouth to convey this information to Mr. Prater, along with anyone else who happened to be listening (which, at the moment, was the entirety of Perkins Cove).

Mr. Prater's face scrunched up. "You mean the boat?"

"No!" Natalie clarified. "The otter!"

"Oh!" Mr. Prater paused to process this. "What a coincidence!"

Isolated chuckles broke out amongst the onlookers, who had otherwise fallen into a hush while waiting in hope of another otter appearance.

Oh, come on, Lars thought. How could they not all see the otter for what she was—a stealing, stinking burglar? Someone who stole valuable, life-giving resources? Who stole the name right off a boat? And, worst of all, who stole *attention*?

Lars felt a growl building up in the back of his throat. Then he felt a bit silly.

Listen to you, he chided himself. *You're being ridiculous. No one's out to steal anything from you. Anyway, I know* some-one *who's stolen a* lot *of fish in his lifetime, and he's that dog you keep seeing in the mirror.* (Lars, like many fully matured dogs, had only recently figured out the identity of the mysterious mirror dog, and was still allowing himself to relish in the personal victory.) *And look how flighty this otter is. Now that she's eaten, I bet she'll probably pass out of here and move on to something else that grabs her interest, and I'll never have to think about her again.*

But it turned out Lars was only half right.

Because Marina, resurfacing a little way away but still well within view, had indeed just found something new to grab her interest.

That new thing was the pod of harbor porpoises who had been hovering, forgotten, at the edge of Perkins Cove.

"No way," Natalie breathed as the crowd rumbled back to life and Diver Bob fumbled frantically to find his phone's video setting. "No way, no way, no *way*."

But it was really happening. Or at least, Marina really wanted it to happen. Slower than before, but still with clear intent and purpose, Marina approached the silvery spectators just beyond the boats. Once she was just a few yards away, she stuck her head up higher out of the water, looking at them with an expression that fell somewhere between curiosity and expectation. After a few moments, her paws came out of the water as well, stroking the sides of her face. Presumably she was just cleaning the fish guts out of her whiskers, but from this far away, it almost looked like she was waving them over.

If she was, it wasn't totally successful. Most of the pod hung back, frozen in the face of this new development.

But Bangor—*classic, friendly Bangor,* Lars thought, with a bittersweet twist of pride in his stomach—swam right up to Marina. She returned the gesture. Now they were mere inches from each other.

Now Marina was leaning over the smooth, curved melon of Bangor's head.

And now...

Puff!

Bangor blew a mischievous burst of air right into Marina's face.

As the humans erupted in laughter and whistles of approval, only Lars's sensitive ears could detect the excited squeak Marina released in response, aimed right at Bangor:

Oh, it's on.

And then they were off, circling the edge of the cove, rolling around each other in dizzyingly tight formation. It was a breathtaking display, the natural result of two of nature's most playful marine mammals coming together. Diver Bob was alternating between dancing with childlike, wondrous joy, and trying to hold the camera steady. Even Adam let out a low whistle of amazement.

And Lars just watched it all from on top of the cooler. There was nothing he wanted more than to jump in the water with them, to join his old friend and, in doing so, maybe even make a new one. But even after a thorough towel-and-shake regimen, Lars could still feel the chill of the autumn ocean lingering in his fur. If he went back in there, it wouldn't be long before that cold burrowed into his bones. And even if he *did* go back in, he knew he wouldn't be able to keep up. He simply couldn't swim as fast as even the slowest otter or porpoise, or turn anywhere near as tightly. And now, as Bangor's siblings gradually decided to join him next to Marina, and the one-on-one play session became a total free-for-all . . .

Well, Lars was happy for them. He really was. Anything that brought Bangor this much happiness, and made Natalie smile this big, couldn't be all bad.

Still, minutes ago, Lars had felt like he was on top of the world. Now he couldn't help but worry that he might still be the odd dog out. And he'd already felt that way plenty before, in those long, dark years he'd spent living rough.

It was the kind of thing you remembered for the rest of your life.

CHAPTER FIVE
Natalie

"Wasn't it the best thing you've ever seen in your *life*?"

These were big words coming from Natalie, who had seen some pretty incredible things. She'd seen the inside of a cloud with her mother at the top of Mount Katahdin, the tallest mountain in Maine. She'd seen the green flash, a rare emerald blaze over the ocean sky, one predawn morning out on the water with her dad. She'd seen that same dad, who had merely nodded in silent approval at the ephemeral beauty of the green flash, jump on a couch and dance when the Bruins squeaked into the playoffs.

And of course, she had seen her best friend and faithful companion, Lars, riding on the back of the very same harbor porpoise who had saved his life. Actually, upon reflection, that had been *really* incredible.

"Okay, *one* of the best things," she conceded, remembering that great day. "Right, Dad?"

"Yes. Sure. Sorry, honey, I'm still kind of in work mode," Mr. Prater grunted, pulling hard at the rope-and-pulley system that allowed him to load tubs full of ice and fish off his boat and onto the dock behind Barnacle Barry's. Customers eating their lunch on the restaurant's waterside patio stopped midbite to watch, delighted by the free show. Presumably they would be less delighted when the coolers came nearer and the fish smell spilled out. But Natalie, whose entire life to date had trained her to associate the smell of fish with loving parental hugs, moved even nearer down the dock to help guide one of those tubs down from the air and onto a well-worn wooden pallet.

"Of course, sorry. How can I help?" she asked. "You need me to wash down the deck?"

"Honey, you're on your lunch break. The operative word there is *break*," Mr. Prater reminded her, stopping just long enough to wipe the sweat off his forehead with his hat. This mostly resulted in him wiping the sweat from his hat onto his forehead.

"Oh, I'm fine," Natalie said, glancing down to the other end of the docks, where Bob still stood at the end of the *Urchin*'s gangway, posing for every family who wanted a selfie. "The next tour's not until two."

"That's not that long from now, Natalie. You need to eat. And how's Lars doing?"

That was a good question. Natalie looked down to where Lars was curled up on the dock, chin poking over the edge as if contemplating the water below, looking oddly subdued for a dog currently surrounded by vast quantities of flying food. Of course, he'd perked up a little right after they'd pulled into shore, when many of those children who wanted their picture taken with Diver Bob had also asked to get one with Lars. Several of them even wanted a picture with Lars *more*. And he'd certainly snapped to attention when Bob had slipped him a treat and said, "Consider this a fantastic initial performance review. For both of you. Natalie, I'll remember to get you your own dog treat next time." Then he'd winked and handed her a piece of chocolate, sending her and Lars off for lunch on a sweet note.

Now, though ... Natalie had to assume her normally exuberant dog was just tuckered out from all that time spent deep-sea swimming. She'd been nervous about overexerting him; otherwise, she totally would have asked Bob if the two of them could go in the water and play with Marina and Bangor while they were still in the cove. In fact, after a few minutes of watching the otter frolic with the porpoises, she'd decided this was too good an opportunity to pass up and vowed to just go for it. But right as she was about to spring into action, Bangor's mother—who Natalie had learned to recognize from the way she always watched cautiously over the pod—clearly decided the porpoises were pushing it and rounded up her family to go cool off somewhere quiet and unseen by human eyes. Seeing her new friends swim out into waters too deep for otters, Marina had turned back to face the humans of Perkins Cove, blinked a few times as if making a decision, and sunk beneath the waves again, with no clear sign of when or if she'd be back. And so Natalie's hopes of an otter-porpoise-dog-girl jamboree had been put on hold for another day.

But Natalie's hopes did not die easy.

"Do you think she'll come back?" she asked her father eagerly. "Do river otters tend to stay in one place? She had to be a river otter, right? I don't think we get sea otters on this side of the country."

"What did Diver Bo—what did Bob say?" Mr. Prater asked, already loading up the next tub of fish.

"I was so excited, and then I was so busy helping everyone off the boat, I forgot to ask." That same excitement was still buzzing through her whole body. Feeling like she had to do *something* with it or else she'd explode,

Natalie hopped down on the boat and went straight for the hose. "But she seemed playful, right?"

"Natalie, your lunch—"

"Wouldn't it be great if she became friends with me and Lars, the way we became friends with Bangor?"

"That would certainly be something."

"What would be something?"

Barnacle Barry appeared on the dock above them, reporting for his daily task of taking the fish away for weighing and crediting.

"Marina!" Natalie said.

Once again, Barnacle Barry looked lost.

"The boat?" he asked.

"The otter." Mr. Prater sighed.

"You renamed your boat after that otter?"

"Wait, you saw the otter?" Suddenly the dock was a popular place to be, because here was Mayor Maher, out of breath and holding what seemed to be an entirely separate cup of coffee from the one he'd been drinking that morning. "What happened? Did we miss it? Who recorded it? Other than half the people in the cove, I mean, based on what's going up online. We need to get on top of this."

"We need to celebrate this!" That was Nancy Jane,

just behind Mayor Maher, clutching a pad and pen and making Natalie smile. Nancy Jane was an artist whose works could be found all around Ogunquit, illustrating the beauty of life along the Maine coast. If there was something as exciting as an otter in town, it was a sure bet Nancy Jane would want to capture it.

When she saw Natalie smiling up at her, Nancy Jane smiled back, reached into her purse, and pulled out a small wax paper bag that she tossed down onto the boat. Natalie opened it and found two cheddar scones.

"I thought these might help keep your energy up between tours."

"Thanks! See, Dad? *Lnchmpf.*" Natalie had meant to say *lunch*, but the moment she'd gotten the scones in her hands, she'd realized she *was* pretty hungry.

"Oh, are you on your break?" Mayor Maher asked. "Great. Because I'd love to ask you how we should start strategizing for when it returns—"

"Strategizing?" Nancy Jane laughed. "John, the otter isn't a *business.*"

"Could be," Barnacle Barry mused. "Look at all those customers on my patio right now. Look at the line for Dugnutt's boat down the way. That's all thanks to Natalie and those porpoises. And this guy," he said, nodding at where Nancy Jane had bent down to scratch Lars's wiry coat. (Lars, for his part, was still sprawled out sullenly on the dock, but he had at least lifted his eyes when the scones had entered the scene.)

"I've been wondering what we should do, too," Natalie confessed. "I've been so busy studying deep-sea life recently, I didn't even *think* to study freshwater animals. There's so much we need to learn—will she be back? Could we work her into the sea life tours? *Should* we? Or should we worry about her being around too many boats, the way we had to with Bangor and the pod? Everyone's been really nice about going slow in the cove and putting pingers on their boats, but do otters need that? And what if she's lost, the way Bangor was? Or—"

"Wait, the otter's a *she*?" Mayor Maher blinked.

"Her name's Marina," Barry explained.

"I thought that was the boat."

"Talk to Mr. Prater. He, like, *spoke* to her."

"To the boat? He does that all the time, I've seen it."

"No, the otter."

"You *spoke* to an *ot*—"

THUD!

Mr. Prater, whose eyes had been firmly glued to the

tub he'd been lifting into the air this whole time, now let it drop so quickly that it shook the dock when it landed, causing both Barnacle Barry and the mayor to jump. Natalie froze, a bite of scone halfway to her mouth, wondering what in the world had gotten into her dad, who was looking back and forth between her and the adults on the dock like someone who found himself outnumbered.

"I did not speak to the otter," he announced, seemingly to the world in general. "I *looked* at her. And, for the record, smelled her. She smells awful. But what I really want to know is: *When* did my family become the official sea life ambassadors of Ogunquit's trade and government?"

Hesitation hung in the air. Barnacle Barry and Mayor Maher looked nervously at each other, or rather, tried very hard to look like they were not looking nervously at each other. Nancy Jane, meanwhile, just kept smiling softly at Lars and petting him gently.

"Well, I wouldn't say *official*..." Mayor Maher said.

Barry threw his hands up and said, "I'm just sayin', *my* daughter doesn't commune regularly with dogs and porpoises. The girl's got a knack, Jim, you know she does."

Natalie turned to her father, trying to swallow the rest of her scone in a way that seemed fitting for a serious conversation.

"I thought you liked Bangor and the pod, Dad," Natalie said. "You taught me to love the ocean—*everything* in the ocean. And we could never have gotten those pingers if you hadn't helped me find those government grant applications. I thought you loved this stuff."

Mr. Prater's hat was back in his hands, and now he was unconsciously wringing it as he tried to figure out what to say next (really wringing it, in this case—with each new squeeze, fisherman sweat dripped from the hat to the deck below).

"Of course," he said at last. "Yes. I've loved sharing those things with you, Natalie. I just . . . we were *just* discussing how busy you are. You remember that, yeah?"

"Yeah," Natalie conceded. "I do."

"And you see how worrying about all this would make you *more* busy, yes?"

"Yes."

"And you know that sometimes you can just see a cute animal and *not* immediately restructure your life around them?"

Natalie paused.

"I don't love that you paused," said Mr. Prater.

Natalie knew that her father was right. She was already stretched thin, and the amount of research she was thinking of doing—not to mention how much she suddenly wanted to spend even *more* time out on the water—would just be piling more commitments on the mountain she already had.

But the sheer joy of seeing Bangor and Marina doing aquatic acrobatics next to each other—to witness that even *one* more time, to *be* in it... wouldn't it all have been worth it?

Seeing her think about this, Mr. Prater knelt next to her on the boat.

"Look," he said. "When Bangor saved Lars's life, it was one of the happiest days of mine. And seeing how much joy those two brought you after, especially with how you were doing with..." His eyes flickered over to the *Searchin' Urchin*, and then to the adults on the dock above them. "With everything with your mother and me... well, I'll always be so, so grateful that Bangor *and* Lars came into our lives. And they helped this town, too. If people online hadn't gone and shared those videos of them playing around our boat, I wouldn't have half the business I do today. But not all attention is good attention."

"You're telling me," Mayor Maher commiserated, no longer even pretending not to eavesdrop. "Half the voters in this town love how we get tourist money all year long now. The other half...not so much. The reporters we've had here, the looky-loos, the, uh, interfacers..."

"Influencers," Nancy Jane said helpfully.

"Thank you...well, some voters miss their peace and quiet."

"Right," Mr. Prater said. "I mean, I'd call them *people* first, not *voters*, but right. And I don't want *you* losing what little peace and quiet you have left, Nat. You give so much of yourself. It's one of the best things about you. But I'd hate to see you give so much of yourself that you forget to give anything...uh...to *yourself*. Just promise that if you need anything, you'll ask for it, okay?"

Natalie looked at her dad, who now seemed doubly exhausted not just by all the hard work he'd been doing, but by all the Emotional Dad Speech Energy he'd had to call up from his inner reserves.

She looked up at Lars, who was staring at her like he wanted something but didn't know how to express it (though this may just have been the scones).

She looked past the mayor's expectant face and over to Bob, who had just seen off the last of the morning's tour-takers and was now walking over to *The Marina*, passing a new line of tourists already waiting for the 2:00 p.m. trip, which would be starting any minute now, with Natalie back on board.

Inwardly Natalie thought, *Honestly, it seems like everyone* else *needs help from* me. But if you were working on things you loved, for people you loved, that wasn't really *work*, was it? She hadn't run this idea by anyone yet, but it seemed right in theory.

Outwardly she said, "Sure thing, Dad. Don't worry." Then she turned to Mayor Maher and said, "And you should tell all those people that more makes merry."

"Hey, that's the thing I always say!" Diver Bob said, just now reaching the group. "Howdy, folks. Hi, Jim. What are we talking about?"

"The otter," Mr. Prater said. "And whether it's Natalie's job to look after it."

"Of course not!" Bob said. "Her only job is helping me on the boat!"

Then he stopped, appearing to reexamine the scene in front of him.

Diver Bob did not have a mean bone in his body, but it would also be fair to say he often seemed more comfortable with folks who *didn't* have many bones in their body, and instead had, say, cartilage, or gelatinous interiors, or fins. He was not always the fastest to pick up on the social cues of land-based mammals. But his heart was in the right place, which accounted for a lot. It accounted for the goodwill he enjoyed around town. It accounted at least in part for the good-natured (if occasionally awkward) relationship he and Mr. Prater maintained, even in the wake of Bob marrying Natalie's mother.

And it helped account for why Bob now made an attempt to clarify: "Well, helping me on the boat *and* making time for her own separate pursuits and good health, of course. Listen, Natalie, if you want to take the rest of the day off—"

I could study for school. Or actually hang out with my swim team friends. Keena and KJ have been suggesting we go get ice cream after practice for weeks now. Or—

"Are you kidding?!" Natalie said. "There's no *way* I'm missing out on another tour! And besides, what if Marina comes back?"

Her father groaned. "Natalie..."

"I'll be *fine*, Dad. I'm too busy to get any busier." This did not seem as comforting to her father as she'd intended it to be, but she pressed on, "And anyway, it's not like one river otter is gonna be enough to cause the press to totally descend on sleepy little Ogunquit. But thanks for worrying about me."

With that, she hugged her dad, who then helped her climb back out of *The Marina*.

After all that fuss, the afternoon tour turned out to be much more run-of-the-mill, with no surprise appearances from high-spirited otters or harbor porpoises. And while a few tourists looked disappointed, Natalie was privately grateful for the chance to just perform her job as normally as possible. She liked making parents feel at ease with her well-honed babysitting skills, and she *loved* making kids laugh by getting into a fake debate with Diver Bob about which end of a sea cucumber was which. Most of all, she loved having Lars there with her, seeing him bask in the children's adoration, and enjoying the way his ears flopped back against his skull when the boat went fast over the water.

When they finally got home to the Praters' shack that night, Natalie knew she should probably do some homework for school or give Lars his usual nighttime walk, but Lars seemed just as exhausted as she was by the exciting events of the day, and they both collapsed into bed within minutes. The last thing Natalie heard before she drifted off to sleep was the sound of Lars barking that bubbling, faraway bark of a dreaming dog. Somehow, Natalie was certain they were both going to dream of otters that night. She smiled, rolling onto her side, pleased to think that Lars's dreams would be just as happy as hers.

The next morning was a Sunday, another workday for Natalie and Lars. This time, when Natalie led Lars in a mad dash back down to Perkins Cove, it wasn't because she was worried about being late. It was because she wanted to see if Marina had returned.

The moment they passed Barnacle Barry's, the answer quickly became clear.

Light and noise filled the air. Cameras flashed. Gasps and exclamations rose up from the waterside. News trucks overflowed out of the parking lot.

The river otter was back.

And the press had totally descended on sleepy little Ogunquit once more.

CHAPTER SIX
Bangor

From the day they had met, Bangor and Natalie had always had a connection. They may have had very different bodies and backgrounds, but when it came to their excitement about making new friends, they were kindred spirits. They knew they were—for lack of a better phrase—mammals of a feather.

But they both would have been surprised to know *just* how kindred their lives were that first day after Marina appeared. While Natalie was attempting to persuade her parent that everything was fine on land, Bangor found himself having a remarkably similar conversation somewhere under the waves off Bibb Rock, a couple nautical miles clear of Perkins Cove.

But your problem is with humans! Bangor was protesting. *Humans and their boats! Not otters! Now you're saying you don't want me going back to play with her?*

Yeah, Bristol chimed in helpfully. *I bet most otters don't even* own *boats.*

Kittery wasn't swayed. *I've encountered otters before*, she clicked. *I know that they're fun, believe me. But they stick close to the shore. Which is where the humans are.*

So do we! Bangor rocked side to side in vexation. *We stick close to harbors!*

Not that *close*, Kittery chirped. *And we've been spending quite enough time near land already. I'm not saying we have to leave—I just want us all to stay away from the cove tomorrow. Give everyone a few days to cool off.*

Bangor couldn't believe what he was hearing. That otter had been almost as fun to play with as Lars. *Almost.* It was a little harder to know what was going on in her head, in comparison to Lars, who was so expressive and open. It was one of the reasons Bangor had felt instantly drawn to him. But the otter was so *fast*—the way she zoomed around Bangor had felt like it was half a dare to keep up, half an invitation to come with.

There was nothing more he wanted than to accept that invitation.

But as he looked around for help from the other members of his pod, he saw that he was floating alone here. Belfast had clearly enjoyed their new playmate, too, but knew he was under thin ice after that stunt he pulled chasing the boat earlier and was playing it safe now as a result. Bristol would have gone back to the Cove in a heartbeat, but as the youngest in the family, her vote held less weight. And Uncle York...well, Bangor wasn't even sure he'd even been listening to the conversation. He was several yards away, savoring a mackerel.

Bangor whistled a long, mournful whistle, signaling his acceptance. Kittery relaxed a little, glad the argument was over. As they all settled in for the night, she brushed up against her son comfortingly, trying to signal that she loved him even when they disagreed. Bangor didn't respond. It was clear no combination of clicks or whistles was going to change Kittery's mind on this.

This was why, Bangor had privately decided, he wouldn't try to change her mind.

He would just sneak out instead.

It is difficult to sneak out when you're a harbor porpoise. For one thing, you're not so much sneaking *out* as sneaking *off*; the ocean is notably low on doors and walls, except around certain shipwrecks. Furthermore, you can't just wait for everyone else to fall asleep, because harbor porpoises never really sleep. Or rather, they do, but not the way other animals do. A harbor porpoise, incredibly, only falls asleep with half its brain at a time. The other half stays awake, allowing the porpoise to keep breathing and stay on the lookout for potential predators. Or, say, misbehaving harbor porpoise children.

A short while later, Bangor contemplated this problem as the rest of his pod rested. When they were half asleep like this, they did zone out a little, but not quite enough. He couldn't just make a break for it; the sudden movement would wake everyone up. Or rather, wake them up more. Since they were, again, technically already awake.

So the trick, then, was to not move, but also to not *not* move.

If this solution sounded like a philosophical riddle, well, Bangor had learned it from the most philosophical porpoise he knew: Uncle York. Sure, Uncle York's philosophy on life was mostly just "swim slowly and eat as much as you can," but it was, undeniably, *a* philosophy, which therefore made York, undeniably, philosophical.

And it was precisely that policy of swimming slowly—*very* slowly—that was about to come in so handy for Bangor. One of the reasons a porpoise always needs half of its brain awake is so that it can keep itself swimming in place, preventing it from floating away from its pod and into the danger of the open ocean. But for several months now, York had been teaching Bangor the secret to his unique swimming technique, the one he'd been using earlier that day. The secret was to not swim at all, and instead let the currents carry you where they may. There was a knack to it. You had to fight against your porpoise instincts to always be in motion and let everything else be in motion around you.

(At least, Bangor had to fight his instincts. He rather suspected this method of life was second nature for York at this point. Possibly even first nature. Having two entire natures probably sounded like a lot of unnecessary effort to Uncle York.)

Whatever the case was, Bangor was about to put this technique to the test. He had positioned himself carefully on the far-right side of the pod, flanked only by his mother on his left. Once he was pretty sure she was resting the right side of her body—the side facing him— Bangor went absolutely still, allowing the current to tug at him, pulling him away, slowly, *slowly*, with such gentle ease he might as well not have been moving at all. And yet, one nautical inch at a time, he was. It was like how you could stare at seaweed forever, not realizing it was growing—but then you would blink, or turn around, and find it had *grown*.

Bangor held his breath. Then he held it some more. Five minutes, six minutes, seven, then eight—he didn't dare push himself up toward the surface for air and risk the motion catching his mother's attention. By the time he hit minute nine, Bangor could feel the biological urge to breathe overtaking him and wondered if maybe this hadn't all been an overreaction, and he could just try and find his otter friend another day.

Then, just when he couldn't take it anymore, the current curved, pushing him around the edge of Bibb Rock. This shielded him at last from his mother's view, or anyone else's in his pod. As quickly and quietly as possible, Bangor shot to the surface for a long, grateful *puff,* followed by a deep, sharp intake of air.

And then he was gone.

It was early morning now. A pink and orange sun rose somewhere far behind Bangor's flukes, casting light forward over his head and then refracting down through the surface of the sea, where the cold of the winter had filled the water with the beautiful green hue of life. Now the colors of the deep and the day met and intermingled, putting on a dazzling light show for Bangor.

Bubbles sparkled like diamonds. Algae shone like emeralds. It all struck Bangor as a sign: *Of course* he was right to go back to the shore. The whole harbor was calling out to him. Who would he have been if he'd resisted?

A good son? Suggested a voice somewhere from the side of his mind. Bangor dismissed this as the side that was cranky from lack of sleep and swam onward.

Before going straight back to Perkins Cove, Bangor had decided to pursue a hunch. Something his mother had said about otters, and where they tended to stay. Just a mile or so north of Perkins Cove, as the cod swam, was another one of Ogunquit's little ports of entry: the mouth of the Ogunquit River, a narrow waterway where several smaller brooks merged and became one fast-running force before emptying out into the ocean. If Bangor's new freshwater friend had come from anywhere, he bet she had come from there.

He slowed down as he approached the river's entrance. Here there were fewer boats on the water and more resort buildings on the shore, looming silently over sandbars and shallow water. It was technically possible for porpoises to swim up freshwater rivers, but the tide was out at the moment, and Bangor didn't think it would be very smart to swim up that slim and rushing stream.

None of this is smart. There was that voice again. *What's your game plan when Kittery looks over and sees you're not there? Especially if the otter's already left town? You'll have done this for no good reason.*

No. Bangor had not come all this way for nothing. She had to be there.

Bangor scanned the water in front of him. But she wasn't in the water.

She was up on the land.

Squiiiishlish! With a sound like a very small rainstorm running across the rocks, a long soft torpedo of fur slid down the slope of the shore. The river otter zoomed on her belly along a slicked-up patch of mud and mulched autumn leaves. When she got to the bottom, just before she would have fallen off a crag and into the water, she pulled out of her descent and scrabbled back up the rocks, only to start the process all over again, squeaking happily to herself the whole way through.

Bangor got the impression that she could have done this all day long. But then she saw Bangor.

The otter froze.

Once more, Bangor was struck by the mystery of her face, the unreadable intentions behind those small dark eyes. Where had she come from? Upriver, presumably, but why had she come here, to the edge of the ocean? Why now? What did she want? Well, left to her own devices, the otter had chosen to spend her time playing. Bangor could relate. But did she want a friend?

All these questions hung in the air like morning mist on the water.

Then Bangor got an answer to at least one question. The otter threw herself off the rocks, into the water, and straight toward Bangor, squealing excitedly as she approached.

For now, this was all Bangor needed to know. He puffed to signal his own excitement, and then shot forward just beneath the surface of the water, racing to meet her midway. They shot past each other, so close he felt her tail brush across the broad side of his dorsal fin. Then they each did their best to come to a halt—a challenge when you were flying free through the ocean—and reversed direction, hurrying at each other once more. There, just beneath the water, those two tiny eyes looked dead ahead at Bangor, not blinking. They got closer to each other, closer, about to collide—

And then, at the exact same time, they both swerved to the side, each of them shooting south and east.

They raced together down the coast, half encouraging each other, half taunting, whirling around each other in twisted twin jet streams. They passed the Lobster Point Lighthouse and Little Beach. They dipped into Oarweed Cove and out again, shocking an early-morning windsurfer. The whole time, Bangor's body felt alive with delirious joy, so perfectly attuned to his bold new swimming partner, and yet so totally mystified by her at the same time. It was intoxicating. It was everything he'd hoped for. It was exactly why he'd had no patience for Kittery's warnings about getting too close to humanity.

Then they rounded a corner and pulled into Perkins Cove.

And got *way* too close to humanity.

CHAPTER SEVEN
Lars

Bright flashes of light burst in the air like a lightning storm at sea level. The morning sun glinted off the painted logos of a whole fleet of local news trucks—and, because this was Maine, local news *boats*, bobbing up and down in a harbor that had become twice as crowded overnight. The last time Lars had seen those boats had been exactly a year ago, when Bangor's pod had first rolled into town and garnered a lot of attention. At the time, press interest had started at a fever pitch and then died off gradually as the news cycle moved on to other things and—in several instances—as the reporters realized that harbor porpoises and dolphins were not, in fact, the same things, and for some reason seemed to be disappointed by this.

(Lars, personally, much preferred harbor porpoises to dolphins. Dolphins could jump impressively high, it was true, but he doubted he would fit on the back of one, so honestly, what was the point?)

Now, though, the press was back, stirred up by those posts on social media that Mayor Maher had mentioned, and that Natalie had scrolled through this morning while wolfing down breakfast. Everyone wanted a shot of the hottest new unlikely friendship to hit Ogunquit— and, judging by all the hubbub, the moment to get that shot had just arrived. With news crews, tourists, and assorted onlookers all jostling one another to get the closest view, it was going to be hard for Natalie and Lars to make it to the dock.

It was about to get even harder.

"Hey, it's them!" shouted someone in a press lanyard, noticing Natalie and Lars. "They're here!"

"I know they're here," grumbled the camera-woman next to her, facing the opposite direction. "I'm trying to get a shot of them through everyone else try-ing to get a shot of them."

"No, not them—*them!* The girl and the dog from last year!"

At this, the camerawoman turned, as did several other journalists nearby.

"Hey, miss! What can you tell us about what's hap-pening here?"

"Natasha, right? Natasha, the porpoise girl? Would

you mind giving an interview to—"

"Lars! Over here! Look at the camera, boy!"

"How did you remember the dog's name?"

"How many dogs do you know named *Lars?*"

His tail wagged involuntarily at the sound of his name, but even an attention-loving dog like Lars found this all a little overwhelming. It was like someone had heard his internal wishes for more of the spotlight and decided to crank up enough spotlight to blind him.

But Natalie, after only the slightest moment's hesitation, straightened up her shoulders, pushed her hair behind her ears, and said, "I'd love to do an interview. How about I just stand over here where the light is better?"

"Of course," said the woman in the press lanyard, stepping aside to let her through and gesturing for everyone else to clear off. "Although actually, the light is—"

Natalie hurried Lars through the newly opened space in the crowd, making a beeline for the dock and leaving the stunned reporters in her dust.

"Things to do! Friends to help!" she called. "Sorry!"

Now Lars's tail was wagging entirely on purpose. For someone who had never adopted a human before, he'd sure nailed it on his first try with Natalie.

Once on the dock, they had a better view of the madness. Out in the water, Bangor and Marina were framed smack-dab in the middle of a half circle of news boats. They weren't trapped—they could have swum back out under the drawbridge if they wanted to—but they were certainly under a *lot* of scrutiny.

Marina, meanwhile, was scrutinizing right back. Like a pinball with paws, she swam in a wild zigzag from one boat to another, pushing up close and then poking her head out curiously. Lars derived some pleasure from watching the humans recoil as she approached, clutching tighter to their cameras and microphones the closer she got. Clearly they had seen the shots of Marina stealing the wares from Mr. Prater's boat, and feared a similar fate befalling their expensive recording equipment.

But then Lars saw something that wasn't so funny. All this chaos was taking its toll on Bangor, who had frozen up in the middle of it all, hiding a few feet beneath the surface like a shimmering mirage.

"Too much noise in the water makes it hard for harbor porpoises to navigate," Natalie muttered under her breath, so soft that only she and Lars could hear it in all the racket. "And none of these news boats know how to adjust for him. He needs help. But what can we do?"

Lars looked up and saw Natalie's problem: Once again, she had worn her wet suit for swimming, but it was buried under layers of warm protective clothing for the blustery boat ride ahead. She couldn't just dump her coat and all her belongings here among all these strangers.

Luckily Lars liked to keep his coat on wherever he went.

Before anyone could stop him, he nosed his way forward, then trotted, then broke into a full-on run. The farther he got down the narrow dock, the more crowded it became, but dogs had ways of moving through crowds that humans didn't. It was all about finding the spaces between the legs. Or, occasionally, making them.

"Ruff!" Lars declared as a public service announcement. "Yarf! *Ruff!*"

Onlookers instinctively shifted or leaped aside. Some didn't have very much dock to leap with, and Lars heard at least one loud *splash* as he raced down the boards. But it wasn't his job to worry about that right now. It was his job to worry about his own, upcoming—

Splash!

Lars threw himself headfirst off the end of the dock

and into the water. He doggy paddled as fast as he could, out past the commercial vessels and through the gaps between news boats. He had no idea where Marina had gotten off to by now, but that didn't matter. He had only one target—Bangor.

Porpoise echolocation sounds are almost always too high for human ears, but Lars could just catch Bangor's clicking if he tried. It was a stuttering sound at the top range of his hearing, and now, as he swam closer, that sound came into focus. Bangor was firing off clicks at a rapid pace, trying to orient himself, but with all these boats in the water, he was only getting more confused. Lars hoped he would pick up on a unique shape that couldn't possibly be confused with anything else: four paws and a panting smile, sloshing their way straight toward him.

The proof of recognition came when Bangor rose to the surface, regarding Lars first with caution and then with clear relief.

Lars intended to keep that relief going. Now that he was closer, he slowed his paddle and allowed the rippling waves to push him gently closer to Bangor until he could nuzzle his nose comfortably along his friend's melon.

"Awwww," said someone in a nearby news boat. "Look! They *are* friends."

The crowd had begun to quiet down. Perhaps, Lars considered, they were all wonderstruck by this moving display.

Then that boat's cameraman said, "We already have video footage of this from last year, boss. This is old news."

"I know, but it's just so *cute*."

Ah. So that's why they'd quieted down. *Well . . . good*, Lars thought, and not just because he was being called cute. He was happy being old news if it kept the noise level down and prevented the press from frazzling his friend.

As if hearing his thoughts, Bangor dipped his head in invitation to Lars—not a deep enough bow to climb all the way onto his back, but exactly low enough for Lars to chuck his chin over Bangor's melon, resting his snout on top of his friend. He did this over Natalie's knee sometimes when she looked like she needed a morale boost or just needed help finishing her eggs, and it seemed to have the same effect now. With his head pressed against Bangor's, Lars could hear the harbor porpoise's heart rate start to stabilize. He was calming down.

Heck, even Lars was calming down. The new position allowed him to paddle less furiously, floating in the waves with his friend's support. This gave him time to stare out at the ocean and think about what was happening. Lars hated seeing his friend stressed out, but privately, he had to admit he was kind of relieved that Bangor still enjoyed his company even with shiny new Marina swimming around. In this moment, there was just Bangor and Lars, the dream team, supporting each other and sharing deep, soothing breaths.

Approximately zero seconds after he thought this, Marina popped back up out of the water, inches away from Lars's face, right on the other side of Bangor. As the humans gasped and cooed, she threw her paws onto the spot just above Bangor's dorsal fin, using him to float as well, and stared at Lars over the porpoise's back like they were two coworkers having lunch across a picnic table. A picnic table that just so happened to be made out of blubber. And was, you know, breathing.

Predictably the humans went nuts.

Cameras flashed and rolled. The air was filled with the loud sounds of anchors (the television kind, not the boat kind). Radio journalists narrated in intense detail. It all added up to a din that made Bangor's heart beat so loudly that Lars could feel it through his chin—and then couldn't feel it at all as Bangor plunged into the water. Lars lurched forward and Marina backed away, startled by the loss of support, as Bangor spun beneath them and finally made a break for it, swimming for the opening of the cove...

Where he was stopped cold by the sight of another, slightly smaller harbor porpoise. Even through the competing aromas of salt water, motor oil, and seaweed, Lars recognized this porpoise's unique scent instantly.

It was Bangor's mother, Kittery.

If it was possible for a harbor porpoise to look stern, Kittery looked remarkably stern. She had announced herself with a puff that could only be described as disapproving, and Bangor seemed as cowed by the one small aquatic mammal in front of him as he did by the army of humanity behind him. So much so that when Kittery turned and started heading back out to sea, she didn't even have to turn around to check that her son would follow. After one last, longing look back at Lars and Marina, Bangor turned and swam off, right on his mother's tail.

"Oh, come on. Did I miss them *again*?"

Lars had been so caught up in the family drama that he hadn't even noticed Natalie approaching, doing a modified breaststroke with her head out of the water for better visibility. A small wake behind her led back to the *Searchin' Urchin*, where Lars assumed she had just run to dump her stuff before joining them. As she pulled up next to Lars and started to tread water, she gazed out through the drawbridge at the Atlantic, where Bangor and Kittery had by now disappeared.

"Well, I'm glad *you* got to see him, at least." She sighed. "Good boy, Lars."

Lars's heart swelled.

"Now, come on, let's— *Whoa!*"

Once again, Marina had burst out of the water—right between Natalie and Lars. Marina spared a brief glance to Lars. Then, seeming to also feel that he was now old news, she spun like a top in the water to lock eyes with Natalie, who had just begun the impossible task of trying to stay frozen while still treading water, attempting not to scare the otter away.

"Hi, uh...hey," she said weakly. "I'm Natalie. You, uh, actually spoke to my dad yesterday? Well, not *spoke* to...I don't know if you even make sounds—"

"*Eep!*" Marina squeaked, and Natalie's jaw dropped.

"You *do*! She spoke to me! Lars, she spoke to me!"

I speak to you all the time, Lars thought. *Sometimes even on command! Big whoop.*

"Do you … want to play?" Natalie hazarded. "I don't know how otters like to play yet, but I'd love to learn."

She fell silent for a moment as if waiting for a response. None was forthcoming. This gave Natalie time to sniff the air.

"Wow," she said. "You *do* smell ba—"

And then she stopped.

Because Marina had just lifted a webbed paw out of the water and high into the air.

Seeing the nonretractable claws at the ends of that paw, Lars couldn't hold back a soft, instinctive growl. If this otter even *thought* about hurting Natalie—

But then Marina just ran the paw slowly down her own cheek, the way she had done yesterday when she first appeared.

Then she lifted her paw up toward Natalie again.

Then she stroked herself again.

"Are you … are you *petting* yourself?" Natalie asked, barely breathing. "Are you showing me how? Do you want me to pet you?"

Again, no response from the otter. But when Natalie

slowly, carefully reached out a hand, Marina didn't move away.

And when Natalie gently ran her palm down the top of Marina's wet, furry head, the otter leaned into the touch.

Natalie finished the pat and then pulled her hand back, speechless.

It was a beautiful, breathtaking moment.

Lars felt heartbroken with jealousy.

Then:

"*Squeep!*" Marina said.

And:

Sploop!

She shot back beneath the waves.

After a few moments of stunned silence, it became clear she had vanished for the foreseeable future. At which point, so did the silence.

"Porpoise girl!" shouted a reporter. "Is it true you named that otter?"

"Porpoise girl, over here! Portland News wants to know—"

"How are we gonna get back to the *Urchin?*" Natalie moaned to Lars as the questions poured in. "These reporters will never let us through as long as they think we have something to say to them."

Lars looked into Natalie's face and saw a girl who was dealing with a lot. It was one thing to be cool and sneak past reporters up on land; it was another to be wet, cold, tired, and looking up at an armada of boats closed around you, all trying to get to you first. Suddenly Lars understood how Bangor had felt just minutes before.

He also understood that he needed to put his own feelings on hold for the moment. His job as Natalie Prater's self-appointed canine companion wasn't to go around being jealous of her petting other animals. It was to make sure she felt good and safe at all times. And right now, that was what he was going to do. These reporters wanted a sound bite? Well, he'd give them one:

"Wroof!" Lars barked, so loudly that some of the journalists jumped, and even Natalie looked startled next to him. "Rorf! Wroof! *Ruff! RUFF!*"

A few reporters tried raising their voices to be heard over the doggy din, but Lars just kept barking and barking as loudly as possible, steamrolling every reporter's questions until one by one they gave up.

"Good boy, Lars!" Natalie grinned. "Look!"

One by one, the cameras were starting to get

packed away as the news crews gave up on getting any usable audio. Still, one or two persistent pundits had stationed themselves right between them and the *Urchin*, and Lars was starting to get tired from all that paddling. For a sinking moment, he wasn't sure if he'd be able to keep this up long enough.

BWOOOOOOM!

With a foghorn blast, a decidedly non-news-related boat pulled up around Natalie and Lars, circling them protectively. It was the *Sammy Boy*, the lobster trawler belonging to Mr. Reardon, head of the Ogunquit Lobstermen's Union, and husband and father to the town's various other Reardons, including...

"Sammy!" Natalie called, waving at the boy up on the edge of the boat.

"Hi!" Sammy yelled back, though his voice was overshadowed by the *Sammy Boy*'s horn on full blast.

The horn stopped briefly as Mr. Reardon poked his head out of the wheelhouse, clutching the ship's mic in his beefy hand. At six-foot-four with a bushy brown beard, he cut an imposing figure as he glared down at the reporters.

"Anchors!" Mr. Reardon roared into his microphone. "Away!"

As the last of the news crews scattered, Mr. Reardon threw down a ladder for Natalie to climb aboard.

"Thank you so much, Mr. Reardon." Natalie gasped once they'd pulled Lars up after her and were steering slowly back toward the dock.

"You're welcome!" Sammy piped up.

"Thank you, too, Sammy. What are you doing out here on your dad's boat, anyway?"

"Our usual babysitter," Mr. Reardon said with a voice like sea ice, "has recently taken a part-time job."

"Ah," Natalie said, blushing through the tattered towel wrapped around her shoulders. "Right."

"Yeah, and Mom's gotta take care of *Cassie*." Sammy pouted. "So I have to be out here with *Dad*."

"Well, don't make it sound like that," Mr. Reardon protested. "This can be fun, right?"

"Yeah!" Sammy said. "I'm gonna make the lobsters fight in a bracket!"

"Maybe not *that* fun."

"Really though—thanks," Natalie said as they slid up toward the *Urchin*. "Everything is getting so crazy so fast. It means a lot to have help—especially your help. I know you were nervous when Bangor showed up last year because you thought it might be a pain having porpoises in a high-traffic area, but look how that turned out!"

"Yes," Mr. Reardon said darkly, his eyes glancing to the crowd on the mainland. "Look how it turned out."

But then he turned to face Natalie head on.

"Of course, I totally agree with you," he said, and Lars felt as surprised as Natalie looked. Mr. Reardon was a highly respected figure in the community, but he distrusted new things on general principles and was not a man to change his mind lightly.

"You . . . you do?" Natalie asked.

"Of course."

Mr. Reardon cut the engines suddenly and the boat came to a lurching halt next to the *Urchin*.

"There's just one thing I hope you realize," he rumbled, a glint of satisfaction entering his eye.

"What's that?"

"*You* get to be the one to tell everyone about this at the next town meeting."

CHAPTER EIGHT
Natalie

Ogunquit had town meetings the way other towns had football games. Some came to play. Some came to watch. But practically everyone attended, and inevitably, some people would butt heads. And for the rest of the week, everyone you saw on the street would have an opinion on what had happened.

This meant a lot of people were about to have an opinion about Natalie Prater. Again.

Including, it turned out, a couple of people she hadn't even expected. Natalie was getting a drink of water from the snack table to prepare herself when she looked up at the stream of people entering the Ogunquit Town Hall and saw Keena and KJ, two twin sisters from the school swim team that she had become close to over the last few months. Seeing their smiling faces, Natalie waved them over and felt herself get giddy—but also a little confused.

"Hey!" she said. "What are you guys doing here? Did you move to Ogunquit?"

Like many of Natalie's classmates, Keena and KJ lived the next town over, in Wells. The two small towns combined were just big enough to support one middle school.

"We came to support you!" Keena beamed.

"Yeah," KJ said. "I heard from Ava on the basketball team that *she* heard from Bella that her older brother John saw a video on his feed that *you* hugged a *sea otter* and *he* heard from his girlfriend who works at Barnacle Barry's that you were gonna tell *everyone* about it at tonight's meeting!"

Keena nodded breathlessly. "So we told our parents we were doing a project on being informed citizens, and they let us come to the meeting!"

Keena's and KJ's parents did not allow them to have phones, and as a result, they had become creative about both entertaining themselves and staying up-to-date on the hottest news. Apparently they were somewhat better at the first part than the second.

"It was a river otter," Natalie said. "And I patted it. Once."

"See? We *really* need to be informed citizens," Keena said gravely.

"Anyway, a pat is like a hug with your hand." KJ shrugged.

"Why didn't you *tell* us, though?"

"I guess it just slipped my mind," Natalie said. Which was true; she'd been so busy researching everything she could about river otters to prepare for this town meeting, she'd hardly had time to think about anything else.

"Well, look who's here!" That was Natalie's mom, appearing behind them to gather a plate of mini doughnuts for herself and Diver Bob.

"Hi, Mrs. Prater," KJ said.

"Hi, Mrs. *Dugnutt*," Keena said, elbowing her sister.

"Hi, Mom." Natalie smiled. What with all the places she had to be these days, she felt like she hardly got to see her mom. Before that, she'd spent a year of her life *purposely* not talking to her mom, right after the divorce. Natalie knew her mother didn't hold this against her—everyone had had a tough time that year—but now that things were more patched up, it only made Natalie feel even more grateful for every chance they got to spend time together.

"Hey, girls." Maria Dugnutt smiled at the three of

them. "How about you all come sit with me and Diver—with me and Bob?"

Natalie wanted nothing more. But looking up at the front of the hall, she saw that Mayor Maher was approaching the podium.

"You guys go on ahead," Natalie said, trying to keep the regret out of her voice. "I'm about to be needed onstage."

"Order! Everyone come to order!" called Mayor Maher to a resounding lack of response. As always, the moments before a town meeting sounded like an orchestra of voices all tuning up at once. Also as always, the mayor's immediate reaction to being ignored was to reach for his gavel and swing it up over his shoulder in order to unleash the *bang* on the podium that would signal that the meeting had officially begun.

But very much *not* as always, Mayor Maher's downswing was interrupted by the extremely odd sound of a hall full of people trying to whisper-yell *"No!"* at the bottom of their lungs.

"What is—I mean, *what is going on?*" Mayor Maher whispered back as Natalie tiptoed up to the side of the stage.

"Cassie is asleep!" someone said, pointing at the front

right corner of the room, where the sea workers had taken up most of a section, the Reardons had taken up half a row, and Cassie Reardon had taken up an extremely comfy napping spot in Mrs. Reardon's lap.

"*So we're just supposed to whisper this whole time?*" the mayor asked exasperatedly.

"No," Mrs. Reardon said, in a normal voice. "She sleeps through talking. It's just sudden loud noises that wake her up."

"Yeah," Sammy Reardon said, with an exaggerated roll of his eyes. "Because she's *inconsistent* about her *values.*"

"Sleeping isn't a value, Sammy," said Mrs. Reardon automatically as if they'd either had this conversation before or one very much like it.

Looking out across the room, Natalie found Keena's and KJ's faces and bit back a laugh when she saw how enthralled they already were by the typical Ogunquit political process. It was fun to get to share this part of her world with some new friends.

At the same time, Natalie was very aware that the stakes for this meeting had just gone from high to higher. If she failed to impress the audience with what she'd learned about Marina, she wouldn't just look bad to

everyone she cared about in this town—she'd look bad
to the people she cared about in the *next* town as well.
More may have made merry, but right now, it mostly
just made her extremely nervous.

She'd be fine. She just needed a moment to take a
deep breath, remember what she'd rehearsed, and—

"Natalie!" the mayor called, and a week of rehearsal
went right out the window. "I believe you have some
things to tell us about Ogunquit's newest resident?"

"I—well—" Natalie couldn't believe it. She was
already freezing up. She knew she should look for
friendly faces in the audience, but right now, looking
at KJ and Keena would just make it worse, which
ruled out her mother and Bob as well since they were
all sitting together. Looking to the front row of
the audience, she found her father giving her a thumbs-
up. But that just made Natalie feel even crummier.
He'd been worried that she was taking on too much. If
she crashed and burned now, that would just prove him
right, and—

"Hold on. *Resident?*" Mr. Grundy, one of the older
fishermen in town, had chosen to kick proceedings
off with Ogunquit's usual feedback process: a completely unasked-for interruption. "So the otter just

103

lives here forever now? How do we even know they'll be back?"

Ah. *That* was more like it. There was something so comfortingly familiar about a grumpy fisherman needing to be sold on something that it snapped Natalie right back into her element.

"Great question," she said. "Technically we *don't* know. River otters can live just about anywhere: inland, on the coast, in ponds, lakes, estuaries—as long as they're in a food-rich environment."

"And what exactly constitutes a—"

"Fish, crab, crustaceans, even frogs. It turns out they're *very* adaptable. Which makes Ogunquit an otter's paradise. So I believe she might stick around."

"Great." Mr. Grundy threw his hands up. "More animals to eat what we fish!"

"One otter is not going to cut into your profit margins, honey," said Mr. Grundy's husband, Saul, owner of the Back Porch Piano Club.

"I don't know about that," said a fisherman a few rows behind them. "I saw one of those porpoises lagging behind the rest recently, and the amount of fish he ate—"

"John, we've heard you talk about this every week,"

said Mr. Reardon. "The amount of fish intake you're describing is simply not possible."

"It happened! I *saw* it happen!"

"Order!" Mayor Maher called out, automatically reaching for the gavel as the bickering started to spiral. "Orde—"

"Cassie!" everyone reminded him.

"Okay!" The mayor huffed and then paused as the room held its breath.

Cassie snored lightly. The room exhaled.

"Does anyone have something more *pertinent* to say?" Mayor Maher asked. "Yes, Jim?"

Natalie's heart raced as her dad stood up. Back when she'd had to convince everyone to let Bangor stick around, he'd been her biggest ally in these meetings. She couldn't wait to hear what he had to say now.

"Listen. I don't know what we're going to do about Marina," Mr. Prater began.

"Wait," said Mr. Grundy. "What's wrong with your boat?"

"What I *do* know," Mr. Prater continued stubbornly, "is that whatever we decide to do, it shouldn't have to be Natalie's job to handle it."

Murmurs broke out. Natalie caught a glimpse of KJ

and Keena gaping at her before she ducked her eyes to the ground, unable to look up for fear of what face she might make.

"I'm fine, Dad," Natalie said, her cheeks flaming red.

"I'm just saying, everyone's putting all this pressure on her—"

"Dad—"

"Of course, of course. You make a good point," the mayor said, either oblivious to Natalie's discomfort or simply choosing to ignore it. "If Natalie is feeling overwhelmed or wants some help, it's more than okay for her to let someone else take the lead on this. There's nothing wrong with advocating for what you want. Goodness knows my constituents do it all the time."

"Yeah?" said Saul Grundy. "Then why don't you practice what you preach and ask Nancy Jane to marry you?"

Murmur, murmur, murmur. Mayor Maher's hand shot for the gavel.

"Cass—"

"Don't you Cassie me!" The mayor hissed. "That remark was way out of line!"

"I mean. We *have* all been wondering when it's gonna happen," Mrs. Reardon admitted.

"I'd be interested to know," Nancy Jane said with an amused smile.

"Me too," said Keena.

"Who *are* you?" Mayor Maher asked haplessly.

"I agree with what Mr. Jim Prater in the front was just saying," said a voice from near the back of the barn.

"*Thank* you," said Mr. Prater and Mayor Maher, for different reasons, presumably.

"I mean," the voice continued, "This is an important issue. Why in the world are we all listening to a thirteen-year-old girl?"

This did not provoke mere murmurings. It provoked mutterings, stammerings, exclamations of protest, and one or two expressions of agreement.

Mr. Prater whirled around, death on his face, and Mayor Maher put a hand flat over his eyes and squinted into the back of the hall. "Who said that?" he asked.

A man with brown hair, glasses, and an impatient expression stepped into the aisle.

It was the man from last week's tour.

"I'm Adam," he said. "Adam Wilson. I just moved to town."

"Welcome to our town, Mr. Wilson," said a voice

like melting steel. "Is there something we're not addressing that you think we should be?"

This came from Natalie's mother, who had shot up out of her seat like someone manning a battle station. Everyone always said it was clear Natalie got a lot from her mom. Growing up, Natalie had assumed they were referring to her wavy dirty-blonde hair and her strong jaw, but watching her mom glare down this newcomer, she suddenly felt proud to be considered similar for a whole other list of reasons.

"Yes," Adam said, seemingly undaunted. "What makes you all think there's just one otter? What happens if it turns out to be an infestation? Are you thinking of someone you might call in to get them out?"

Okay. Back to grumpy questions. Natalie could handle grumpy questions. This was her chance to regain control of the proceedings. She cleared her throat, and all heads swiveled to her like she was up to bat in the bottom of the ninth at the World Series.

"For starters," she began slowly, trying to make sure her answers were airtight, "we could try to find her—or their—den."

"How?" Adam asked.

"Well..." She was picking up steam now. "Any river

otter around here probably isn't actually living in Perkins Cove. They tend to live in areas of clean water, near fallen logs, and especially in or near old beaver dams. There's a few up the Ogunquit River not far from the shore."

"How not far are we talking?"

"One mile, maybe two. An otter's home range can be as small as three square miles."

"Yeah," Adam said. "Or as big as sixty."

Who *was* this guy?

"And what will you do if you find this den?" he continued.

"Well, if we find them, we can do a better job protecting them," Natalie said. This got nods of approval from around the room, including an emphatic one from Mr. Prater, who seemed to have entirely forgotten that he was undermining his daughter's authority the second someone else decided to undermine his daughter's authority.

"We could even set up local ordinances for fur trapping in that area," Natalie continued. "A quarter of otters who get trapped in Maine are accidentally caught by people looking for beaver."

"Marina might get *trapped*?" Sammy Reardon gasped.

"Sammy, you've helped me trap lobsters all week," Mr. Reardon pointed out. "These things happen."

"Oh, right." Sammy mulled this over. "But we don't trap porpoises, right?"

"Of course not. The porpoises are protected by law. And if we really wanted, we could probably do that for Mari—for the otter."

"Do you know where the porpoises live?" Adam cut over Mr. Reardon to ask this, and something about the way he did it made the hair stand up on the back of Natalie's neck. But she would not be fazed by this creep. She was Natalie Prater, and she was her mother's daughter, and she was—fine, why not—the porpoise girl.

"Their location shifts," she said. "When Bangor first came here he would stay right in the cove, but now that the whole pod's here, they're usually spotted to the north, a little more out of the way of the boats."

"But do you know *specifically* where?" Adam asked.

Then he turned toward Natalie's mom, pointing his gaze down at Diver Bob.

"You seem to know," Adam said. "Since you drove the boat straight to them."

"They tend to come to us, actually," Bob said. His

perfectly pleasant tone reflected either a complete inability to pick up on social cues or a skill for handling them that Natalie had never witnessed before. "I think they're drawn to the sound of Lars barking."

"Maybe," Adam said. "Or maybe it's all that fish you feed them. Do you find they've responded well to being trained to rely on humans?"

Now Bob frowned. The frown looked uncomfortable on Bob's face, like it wasn't used to being there and was hoping it might get to leave soon.

"I'm not—"

"This meeting is about the otter," Mayor Maher cut in. "Not the porpoises. Does *anyone* have any more questions about the otter?"

"How soft is she?" asked Keena, who was taking to town meetings like a duck to water.

"Very soft," Natalie said, smiling.

"How do you suggest we find this den?" Nancy Jane asked.

"*Thank* you, dear." Mayor Maher exhaled, in a clear moment of true relief. Then someone in the back whistled "Here Comes the Bride," and his forehead began to throb again.

"I could go looking for her," Natalie said. "I know a

lot about the signs of a den now. Maybe Lars could even help us find her. She has a *really* strong scent—it can't be hard to pick up."

"Great idea!" Mayor Maher said, perking up at this clear action item the way a drowning sailor might perk up at a lifeboat. "When would you like to do it?"

"We have school off on Friday," Natalie said. "I could do it then."

"Friday afternoon you have a tour," Bob reminded her. "Sorry."

"Oh yeah." Natalie flushed. "Friday morning?"

"No, Friday morning you're babysitting for us," Mr. Reardon said. "Not sorry."

"I could come with her!" Sammy suggested.

"It's safer than being on a lobster boat." Mrs. Reardon sighed.

"Natalie, I just think..."

Natalie's heart stopped as her father stood up one more time. *Please, no,* she quietly willed, staring at him. *Let me prove I can do this. Please. Please understand.*

Mr. Prater looked up into his daughter's eyes. And while he may not have understood everything, he seemed to understand *something.* Because now he said, "I just think . . . Lars might have an easier time scenting for Marina if he has something that smells like her. She ran across my jacket when she got on my boat, and it *still* smells like her. I'll lend it to you."

Natalie smiled gratefully. Her father tried to smile back, but it wasn't very convincing.

Mayor Maher's smile, on the other hand, was so big he could have swallowed his tie. "Great!" he boomed, practically giddy at the prospect of bringing this meeting to a close. "It's a plan! Meeting *adjourned*!"

In his excitement, he grabbed the gavel.

Bang!

"Waaaaaaaaa!"

"Sorry, Cassie." He sighed.

A few minutes later, townsfolk wandered out into the night or lingered around the snack table. Natalie's mom, dad, and stepdad were all clustered in the corner, talking among themselves, with Mom and Dad throwing dark looks around the room that indicated they were looking for Adam Wilson. Natalie stood on her toes to try to find him as well but failed to do so before Keena and KJ barreled up and gave her a heel-rocking twin hug.

"You did great!" Keena said.

"Especially with that jerk in the back!" KJ said. "Town meetings are high key *wild*!"

"Do you want help finding the otter den?" Keena asked. "We're free then, too!"

"Yeah! Or we could help watch that loud kid you babysit!"

For a moment there, Natalie had been overjoyed, but now she felt flustered. Did the twins think she couldn't do it herself? She didn't know them very well yet and dreaded coming off as needy. Well, she'd show them she wasn't.

"Actually I'll be fine," she said. "I can babysit Sammy and find the otter's den at the same time. You guys can sleep in that morning. And then . . . you can both join me on Diver Bob's boat tour in the afternoon and see me and Lars at work!"

Natalie surprised herself even as she was saying it. What was she thinking? Wouldn't that just add *more* pressure to Friday? But the twins looked so thrilled at the idea that if she backed out of it now, she'd *definitely* seem like she couldn't handle herself.

"You're amazing!" Keena said, checking her watch. "Oops—it's time for our parents to pick us up. See you Friday!"

Natalie watched them bound out into the night, just like Adam Wilson had done earlier, apparently. What *was* that guy's deal? Why had he moved here? Did he even have a kid? If not, why had he been on that boat tour? And *why* was he so interested in the pod?

Oh, well. She wouldn't let him get to her. She wouldn't let anything get to her. She didn't need help from anyone.

Except maybe from Lars.

CHAPTER NINE
Lars

Lars *really* didn't want to help.

It wasn't even because he was jealous of Marina. Really. It wasn't.

Well. Maybe a little bit. The whole town had been buzzing about her all week. They'd also been buzzing about Lars and Bangor, true, but with way lower levels of buzz.

More than that, though, there was one, way bigger, genuinely far more pressing reason Lars did not want to help Natalie find Marina's den. Because if the faded scent coming from Mr. Prater's jacket smelled this strongly and this bad a whole week later, then finding Marina's den might actually make Lars's nose fall off his face.

"Come on, Lars," Natalie begged, dangling the jacket just in front of his snout. "Do you smell that? Do you think you can find more of that smell?"

Could he? Yes. Would he? The jury was still out.

Lars jerked his head this way and that, trying to avoid the jacket.

They stood on the riverside at the mouth of the Ogunquit. Looming up behind them was the Marginal Way, the beautiful seaside path they'd taken to get here. Up on the Way, the world smelled like sea spray and the continental breakfasts wafting out of the backs of coastal resorts.

Lars would have given anything to be back up there.

"Maybe you should throw the jacket," Sammy Reardon said. "And see if he fetches it."

"We don't want him to fetch the jacket," Natalie said patiently, giving it a little shake. "We want him to fetch... to find... whatever *smells* like the jacket. An unused beaver den, probably. Or a used one, I guess, if she's there now."

Lars looked Natalie straight in the eyes and whimpered as pathetically as he possibly could. *I don't want to find anything that smells like this otter. Including this otter.*

But then he kept looking at his human's eyes and noticed something: There were big gray bags under each, and they were very, very tired. Something must have happened at the town meeting, because when Natalie and Mr. Prater had come back to the shack that night, she'd refused to talk to her father. Since then, she'd been staying up extra late to do all her homework *and* research local trapping laws as if determined to prove she could accomplish both tasks. In a way, she'd succeeded; she'd proven she could accomplish both tasks as long as she didn't accomplish any sleep. Now, watching her try to brave her way through exhaustion to be a good babysitter to Sammy and a good friend to animals everywhere, Lars felt his heart roll over and play dead in his chest.

Here, his heart told him, was a girl who needed a win.

And here, at the end of the day, was a dog who wanted nothing more than to help her win.

Darn it.

Fine.

Lars sighed internally, and then—because he didn't want anyone thinking he was *eager* to do this—slowly raised his haunches, shook out his fur, and lowered his front legs to the ground in a *biiiig* stretch. Then, when he felt properly limbered up and waited upon, he straightened out, sniffed the air, and began to move up the banks of the Ogunquit River. With a cry of surprise, Natalie and Sammy moved to follow him.

Oh, Marina had been here, alright. Every day this

week, by the smell of it. The whole place reeked of her, her scent trails crisscrossing back and forth across the banks like some sort of big black dotted line that only Lars could see, made out of mischief and day-old catfish guts. But rather than follow the crazy tangled path of every scent line, Lars was following the overall *trend* of the lines, which led them farther and farther up the side of the river.

At first this meant walking along the bottoms of scrubby sand dunes; here at the mouth of the river, they were technically walking along the edge of Ogunquit Beach, and tourists or retirees out for an early-morning walk waved to the trio from up on the dunes as they passed by below. Then, after they took a footbridge over a sweeping salt marsh, the broad path of the river started to narrow down into a smaller stream, winding westward and leading them inland, away from the ocean. Gradually, wide flat wetlands gave way to steeper slopes of rocks, trees, and underbrush, bordering them and providing shade.

As Lars led the way, moving slowly so the kids could keep up, Natalie and Sammy got to talking behind him.

"So," Natalie said at one point, "how're things at home?"

"Good," said Sammy, who had shown up dressed for today's outdoor activities in a floppy sunhat, wrap-around sunglasses, tube socks stuffed into Crocs, and a pocket-laden fishing vest that he had clearly taken from his father's closet, and which dragged along the ground when he walked. Every few minutes, he would pull a new granola bar out from a new pocket, take a few bites, and then toss some ahead to Lars. Lars didn't want to sound dramatic, but he would have died in the heat of battle for Sammy Reardon.

"It was nice of your dad to help out Lars and me the other day," Natalie said.

"Yeah. He likes you guys," Sammy says.

"Really? Sometimes I kind of feel like he thinks everything that happens in this town is my fault, and it's my job to fix it."

"*That'sh* how you know he *likesh* you," Sammy said, and then swallowed some granola bar. "If he didn't, he wouldn't think you could fix it."

"Hmm." Like many dogs, Lars could smell human moods, and the smell of pride and quiet satisfaction was rolling off Natalie now. Something about this worried him, but he was too busy focusing on keeping Marina's scent in his nostrils to tease it out.

"And how's the rest of your family?" Natalie asked.

Sammy didn't respond, but a scented plume of irritation went up over his head like a mushroom cloud.

"Hmm," Natalie said again when the silence had lasted a few dozen yards. "Is this possibly about Cassie?"

"*Everything* is about Cassie!" Sammy yelled, throwing his little hands up. "She comes out of nowhere one day and suddenly everything in life revolves around her! Everyone only wants to pay attention to *her.* And it's like, why? We barely even *know* her. She can't even *talk.*"

Preach, thought Lars. *That sounds awful.*

"She does talk, though," Natalie said. "She calls Lars *doggy* all the time."

"Yeah, like a *baby.*"

"I mean, she *is* a—"

"And you know what else she does all the time? *Cries.*"

"You know, crying is a form of communication, too," Natalie said. "When a one-year-old cries, it can be a sign that they don't know how to ask for help, but they want to. Asking for help when you need it actually sounds pretty mature, to me."

Really? Lars thought. Could Natalie not hear how she sounded? Clearly the situation she was describing was just like hers, but somehow, she didn't seem able to connect the dots.

"I just think Cassie should go back to where she came from so that things can go back to how they were, and people can have time for me again."

Whereas Sammy, on the other hand, was clearly a very perceptive young man.

By now they were almost a mile and a half up the river. The smell was still there, but the morning was dragging on, and Lars was starting to wonder just how far they might have left to go. He had the energy to press on for hours, but Sammy was young, and Natalie was tired. He didn't want to exhaust the humans that fate had placed in his care.

Natalie seemed to have the same thought, because she squinted up at the sky and said, "We should turn back soon. I don't want to be late for the tour. And there's some dark clouds moving in from the east."

"But what about Marina?" Sammy asked.

Natalie shrugged.

"Even if we don't find her," she said, "we learned that she *is* up here. Either that, or Lars just led us on a wild goose chase."

Lars bristled at the implication that he might not be

delivering grade-A scent work. Even now, where Marina's scent line had begun to interweave with scents of beaver, porcupine, and white-tailed deer, he was still managing to pick her specific stench out of the lineup of—

Wait.

Beaver.

An unused beaver den, probably.

Lars sniffed the air and set off once more, but this time, he went full speed ahead. The excitement had gotten to him. He was really on the scent, now.

The scent of beaver.

Behind him, he heard Natalie holler, run forward after him, pause, and run back to take Sammy's hand and help him keep up. Then the three of them were moving together, scrambling around rocks, pushing past low-hanging branches, and leaping over fallen logs.

More and more fallen logs, actually. Whatever patch of the river they had reached, it was dotted along the side by gnawed stumps, the kind you might find if a beaver had been around, restructuring the riverside into the shape of . . .

A den!

"Whoa," Natalie breathed.

There, where the slow-moving brook met the bank, was a pile of interlaced pieces of wood, covered in teeth marks that signaled a beaver was here. To Lars, the residual smell of the American beaver signaled this as well. But there was a second, more recent, much stronger, much worse smell that hovered all around them—so strong he wouldn't be surprised if even the humans could smell it.

"Marina," Natalie said. "She's been living right here. I was right!"

"*Cool.*" Sammy knelt down to look inside, instantly soaking the bottom of his father's fishing vest in the edge of the stream. "She's not here. But look! You can see where she's been!"

Natalie knelt too, and Lars slyly positioned himself between the two crouching humans, squinting into the shady space beneath the branches.

"Check it out," Natalie said softly, pointing at the mud inside the den, which was crisscrossed with paw prints. "All the tracks are the same size, and they all go to one sleeping area—too tiny to be a whole family's. I think it's just her here."

"You mean she's alone?" Sammy asked.

Natalie nodded. "Seems like it."

"No wonder she wants to play with Bangor and everyone else. She must be lonely."

Okay.

Lars hadn't thought about that.

He'd only thought of Marina as a social darling, adored by everybody. But that was only when she came to the cove. Out here, up along the river, she was just as alone as Lars had been for all those terrible years of being a stray. Natalie had mentioned that otters often moved as families, so he knew this wasn't the norm. How did Marina feel about that—about being an outsider?

Lars knew how he'd felt about it. It hadn't felt good.

For a second, Lars began to see Marina differently.

Then he just started to see her, period.

Because she had popped up from behind a particularly large fallen log a few feet away and was staring right at him.

Lars went stock-still, every muscle in his body tensing up. In the process of doing so, he pushed up against Natalie, accidentally getting her attention.

"What—" she began, and then looked up where he was looking.

"Oh my— *Sammy.*" She hissed.

Sammy looked up, squealed, and then immediately clapped his hands over his mouth. They all froze, wondering if the sudden noise would drive Marina away.

Instead she came closer, slithering over the roots and rocks until she was just a foot away from all of them.

Surprising everyone, but especially himself, Lars stepped forward from between Natalie and Sammy to greet her.

Otter and dog studied each other. Lars looked in her eyes for a hint of those feelings he knew all too well. Did he detect loneliness there? Hope? A soul reaching out for connection? For—

Marina turned around, stuck her butt in Lars's face, and rubbed it all over him, covering him in pure, unmoderated otter smell. Then she jumped into the river and swam off toward the coast at high speed.

For a dog, for whom sense of smell was everything, it was like living through the apocalypse. It was like having your world lit on fire, and also having that fire be made out of garbage.

And it was making Natalie and Sammy *laugh*.

"I can't believe it," Natalie said, doubled over, her T-shirt over her mouth. "I can still smell her on you! I didn't even know they could *do* that! Oh, Lars, I'm so sorry!"

"It's like a skunk made out of *fish*!" Sammy screamed with delight, even as he plugged his nose.

"Wait till I tell Diver Bob about thi— Oh, *Bob*!" Natalie's eyes widened. "Now we're *really* gonna be late! We have to go!"

"Shouldn't we wash Lars first—"

"There's no time! Let's go, Sammy, come on! I'll carry you!"

"I'm not a *baby*!"

"Okay, then keep up!"

And they charged on up the stream, leaving Lars to run after them, utterly speechless in a devastated daze.

This was what he got for helping.

CHAPTER TEN
Bangor

This is what I get for letting us stay here, Kittery clicked. *For letting you come down to this town. Twice! Even after I saw how crowded it was last year!*

Three times, Bangor protested. Some part of his brain knew correcting his mother was a bad idea, but, well, maybe that half of his brain was asleep right now. *I've come down here for three winters now, and clearly no one has gotten hurt!*

You may have come here three times, Kittery clicked with quick irritation, *but I've only let you come here twice. The first time, you did it without my permission.*

That was an accident! I got separated from you!

Yes! And it terrified me! And I never want it to happen again! And last week, when I looked over and you weren't there? I thought it had!

It was the same fight they'd been having every day since Bangor had snuck off to find Marina— and the entire press corps of southern Maine. From the moment Kittery had gotten him away from the madness, she'd wanted them to go right back up to the northern gulf and stay there for the rest of the year. Or, possibly, forever. And while being ambushed by all those humans had shocked him, too, Bangor knew that his best chance of ever seeing his Ogunquit friends again was to double down on remaining here.

And so they fought.

Belfast, Bristol, and York all floated a respectable distance away, letting mother and son hash it out together. Occasionally Bristol would lurch forward, seemingly wanting to speak up for peace, but Belfast would swoop around fast enough to fence her in where it was safe.

You don't want that heat, little sis, Bangor distinctly heard his brother whistle.

She was waiting for me! Bangor cried, not for the first time, picturing Marina's face. *She clearly wants someone to play with.*

You know who else was waiting for you? Every human alive! What if one of those boats had hit you? What if one of them had wanted to hunt *you? To take you away?*

These humans don't do that—

YOU DO NOT KNOW ALL OF THESE HUMANS!

The clicks hit like concussive blasts, practically rolling Bangor backward through the water. By the time he'd regained his balance, it was clear a new technique was needed.

Okay. I'll admit it, he chirped softly. *I was scared when I saw all those boats. I couldn't hear where I was going. And even though you were mad when you showed up, I was still happy to see you.*

This appeared to make Kittery soften a little. Bangor continued:

But maybe if we'd stuck around, worked together—

Sticking around humans is exactly what we don't *do*, Kittery emphasized with a flap of her tail. *Have you ever thought you should listen to your* fear?

Have you ever thought you should listen to joy?

Bangor's words made Kittery pause and regard her son.

I do, she clicked finally. *Every day. When I spend time with you.* Then, before turning away, she added, *But I guess you don't feel the same way about your family.*

No—Mom—

But she was swimming out to the deeper ocean, getting her space, and giving Bangor space of his own.

It should have felt great, like getting exactly what Bangor wanted.

It felt terrible.

Come on, Bristol, Belfast said. *Let's go look for a blue lobster, yeah? Those are cool, right?*

O...kay. Bristol looked back at Bangor once before swimming off.

Which meant everyone had left.

Well, except for Uncle York. But Uncle York didn't really have to leave a place to seem like he was checked out.

Which was why Bangor was so surprised when his uncle clicked, *I know how you feel, you know.*

You do?

Of course, York whistled lowly. *I love my me-time. Pursuing my own passions.*

But you're always with us, Bangor pointed out. *You're never alone.*

Me-time doesn't have to be alone. Have you ever noticed I'm always following something?

Yeah. Schools of fish. Bangor wasn't sure where this was going.

No. You. York was dead serious. *I follow all of you, everywhere. I don't* have *to do that. But I like to. I value my me-time, yes. But it's better because it's underlined by* you *time. All-of-you time. The safety and comfort I feel with you all, with my family . . . it makes me feel good enough to pursue the goals I most deeply care about.*

There was a pause.

Like devouring schools of fish, York clarified.

That's . . . incredibly sweet to hear, Uncle York, Bangor clicked.

Yes. Well. It's a sweet thing to feel.

Uncle York, Bangor realized now, was drifting away slowly. He'd been doing it this whole time, but since he'd been using the no-swimming swimming technique, Bangor hadn't even realized it was happening. Uncle York could surprise you like that.

So maybe if you ever feel that sweet thing yourself, Uncle York continued, *you could let your mother know. I'm sure she'd love to hear it, too.*

And then he was floating off, and now Bangor was alone.

He didn't even realize he was swimming back to the mouth of the Ogunquit River, where he'd last met Marina, until he had arrived there at the tip of the beach.

There was no sign of Marina up on the rocks.

Once again, though, it turned out he'd just been looking in the wrong place. Because here she came now, bounding out of the mouth of the river, racing and squeaking along the banks as if under distress, or even under chase.

Bangor liked to think he was slowly getting better at reading the otter's face. But on second thought, maybe he wasn't, because the look he thought he saw now shocked him with recognition. It was the look of someone who'd just had the comfort of their home taken from them, who'd felt driven to run and run until they barely knew where they were.

Marina looked exactly how Bangor had felt the first time he'd ever wound up in Ogunquit.

But that couldn't have been correct. Because when Marina got to the top of the rocks, she stopped, groomed her whiskers, and calmed down. It was as if she was letting the stress wick off her like seawater off her waterproof fur. She started to slide, which decided it: *Surely* this independent creature couldn't have been as upset as Bangor had thought she was.

Right?

Once again, Bangor puffed to signal that he was

nearby and happy to help out if Marina wanted a playmate.

Marina looked up, squinting in Bangor's general direction. Bangor was beginning to get the idea that river otters were pretty nearsighted.

He flashed some dorsal fin as he swam up closer, trying to communicate: *Hey! It's me! Your friend is here!*

Marina considered this.

And then Marina ran away, up the rocks and over the land, where Bangor couldn't follow.

Where she'd be even more alone than before.

The last time Bangor had watched Marina play on those rocks, he'd thought about how she made her own fun when left to her own devices. This time, a new thought occurred to him: Marina sure seemed to be left to her own devices a *lot*. Maybe it was less that she liked to make her own fun...and more that she *had* to.

As thoughts about York and Marina swam around inside his melon, Bangor wanted to go back and find his mother so he could tell her about all this. But he didn't know if she'd want to see him right now, given how mad she was. Which made him sad. Which made him want to play with Marina or Lars. But they weren't his real family, and they were nowhere to be found right now.

And so Bangor floated sadly away from the shore, caught at the edge of two worlds. And as a cold October rain began to dapple the water above him, he started to worry that by trying to have two families, he might have ended up with none.

CHAPTER ELEVEN

Natalie

Once again, Natalie was exhausted on a boat.

Once again, as that boat pulled out of the harbor, she prepared for a cool, refreshing blast of ocean air to remind herself that everything was basically fine.

But she was standing downwind of a wet dog who smelled like otter musk and, well, wet dog; she was in charge of a young boy who was rapidly crashing from a frantic run fueled by sugary granola bars; and she found herself in front of a boat full of expectant passengers waiting for her to do or say something entertaining.

And it was starting to rain.

If she was being totally honest, things had been basically finer.

It wasn't just the usual tourist families who were sitting there watching her, either. Keena and KJ were right there in the front row. And behind them, back for a second tour—because of course, *of course*, he was back for a second tour—was Adam Wilson. Natalie would have loved to ask him why he was here, but it wasn't a good look to confront one of the customers in front of all the others, and in any case, they were already running ten minutes late, and she had a job to do. Just a couple minutes ago she'd run up to the dock, panting, with Sammy's sweaty little hand in hers, to be ushered on by a smiling but confused Diver Bob. Now Bob was in the wheelhouse, piloting them out of the cove, and Natalie was supposed to be putting a life jacket on a cute and helpful dog.

Except the dog currently sitting on the cooler was too stinky and miserable to be very helpful, and frankly, Natalie was worried about getting the otter smell on the life jacket.

"Who wants to see me put a disposable rain poncho on a dog?" she asked, trying to make this sound equally fun.

"Me!" said KJ and Keena at the same time. The rest of the boat was silent.

This more or less set the tone for the rest of the tour.

"It's, uh, it's dangerously hard to tell which end of a sea cucumber is which," Natalie stuttered lamely into the microphone, a dreary half hour later, as Bob brandished the slimy thing high for all to see. She dimly recalled discussing this topic last week, causing children and even a few parents to roar with laughter. This week, though: "This is, um, funny," she clarified, "because, uh, it shoots water out of its butt."

Nobody laughed, but at least Sammy—poor, tired Sammy—perked up for the first time all tour.

"Hey," he said. "That's kind of like what happened to Lars. But with smell."

"That's right!" Natalie said.

"Pardon me, young lady," said one concerned mother, raising her hand meekly, clearly not an Ogunquit citizen. "Why *does* your dog smell like...I mean, what happened to him?"

Okay. Turn this around. What would Bob say?

"He smells bad today..." Natalie began, trying to spin it into a fun story, "because today we met... Marina! The river otter of Ogunquit!"

Now everyone on the boat was paying attention—including the twins.

"You did?! Is she here now?" KJ asked.

"Well, uh...no," Natalie admitted. "We found her back on land, at her den. But then she ran away."

The crowd began to deflate, except for Adam, who puffed up.

"Yeah?" he snorted. "Bet she's terrified to go back to her home now. Now we'll *never* find out where she is."

"Why do you even—" Natalie began, at which point Diver Bob said, "Who wants to shake hands with a lobster?!"

A scattering of kids indicated wary interest. Diver Bob flashed Natalie a look that said *Let's stay focused, huh?* It came with a smile, but it was still a shock. Natalie didn't even know her stepdad *could* flash looks.

And Marina wasn't the only one missing.

"Where are the dolphins?" asked one child. "Are they coming?"

"They're harbor porpoises," Natalie said.

"Oh! Are *they* coming?"

"Great question," Adam said. "*Are* they?"

"I'm . . . not sure."

But the answer was: probably not. Nobody had seen the pod since the big press fiasco last week. And with Lars remaining sulkily silent in the corner, they couldn't rely on him barking any invitations.

"Wait, is Bangor not coming?" Sammy asked. "That's *boring.*"

"Well, we *never* know if Bangor and his family will

come join us or not," Natalie said, trying to mirror Bob's relentless good cheer. "But Diver Bob's been running this tour for years without any porpoises, and I think it's pretty fun, anyway."

"I already *took* this tour." Sammy pouted.

"You *never* know?" Adam asked skeptically. "There's no way of knowing where they'll be?"

"I mean, they have tags on their fins," Natalie said. "From sea labs up and down the coast. Marine biologists keep track of them. That's actually where their names came from: Bangor, Belfast, and all those other towns with labs."

"Huh. Interesting," Adam said. "So there *would* be a way to find them if you knew someone at those labs. And the only way they could *truly* get lost is if those tags somehow got removed."

Again, Natalie wanted to ask: What on earth was this guy's deal? But she knew that asking that out loud would only send this tour completely off the rails.

"What on *earth* is your deal?" asked Keena.

Wearily Natalie reflected that the problem with boats was they were never on rails to begin with.

"I beg your pardon?" Adam scoffed.

"You come to the town meeting and start attacking

140

our friend, you come on this tour—which is for *kids* by the way, *weirdo*—"

"Diver Bob's Sea Life Tours are for all ages," Diver Bob hurriedly assured the handful of shocked parents.

"And you ask all these weird, mean questions," Keena continued. "Who *are* you? What did you even move here for?"

"I'm interested in sea life," Adam said tersely. "This is a great town for it."

"Then you'll *love* our touch tank!" Diver Bob said, lowering a large tub full of sea stars, scallops, and shells into the middle of the deck. "Go nuts, kids—*of all ages*!"

Normally the touch tank didn't come until much later in the tour, since the excitement of petting all those creatures pretty much shot any chance you had at getting the kids to sit back down in an orderly fashion. But Diver Bob's gambit worked masterfully. Right now, a bunch of happy, chattering kids was *much* better than a bunch of kids sitting quietly, listening to history's most awkward guided tour.

"In a few minutes, we'll return the creatures to the water," Diver Bob said quietly to Natalie. "Then we'll return to land. Sound good?"

As an end to her suffering, Natalie thought it sounded amazing. As a confirmation that she'd completely blown it, it sounded awful.

But there was one last humiliation left in store for her before the tour was over.

At first, it seemed like it might be the tour's saving grace.

As the *Urchin* pulled back into Perkins Cove, carrying a boatload of confused, cranky, and generally damp passengers, no one had much of anything to say. Even the normally talkative Sammy just slumped his head over the railing and watched the stormy sea pass by with the kind of melancholy usually reserved for art school students and long-haul truckers.

Then, from the other side of the boat, KJ released an overjoyed cry, followed almost instantaneously by Keena:

"It's Marina! She's there by the drawbridge!"

Everyone turned or jumped off their seats to look, and sure enough: There, poking out of the water just ahead, were the comically long whiskers and pink little tongue of Marina's adorable otter face.

Natalie couldn't believe her luck. She grabbed for the microphone and began narrating as quickly as she could. "If you look just up ahead, you'll see the famously playful North American river—"

But she hadn't narrated quickly enough, because within moments, she was drowned out by someone else with something to say:

"YARF! WARF! WROOF! WOOF! RUFF! RARF! ARRARRARRF! WRUFF!"

Lars, practically throwing himself over the railing, had unleashed a storm of invective on Marina so fierce, so loud, and so startling that the closest parents pulled their kids away from him, and a boy in the very back row started to cry.

"Lars! No! *Bad dog!*" Natalie snapped, trying to yank Lars off the railing. But he'd hooked his two front paws in stubbornly, determined to give Marina a piece of his mind.

The otter just looked up at him, ran her fuzzy paws over her whiskers—and plunged back into the waves, failing to emerge again. Lars kept barking for several minutes afterward, just in case she hadn't heard him.

Thus ended the tour.

Back on land, passengers disembarked in varying states of misery. Parents muttered. Children sniffled. Sammy trudged up the dock to where his little sister and mother waited for him, the latter asking, "Is that your father's fishing jacket?" Adam Wilson rolled his eyes and grumbled something under his breath as he passed Natalie on the gangway.

But the worst of all was Keena and KJ. Because they weren't grumbling or rolling their eyes at all. And that made Natalie feel crummier than anything else.

"It's really fine," KJ said.

"Yeah!" Keena agreed. "We got to go on a boat! That's so cool! Our parents don't take us on boats! They're just, like, realtors."

Natalie wanted to answer them, to tell them this wasn't the real her, that she wished they would just forget everything they saw today. But if she started talking, she was worried she might start crying. So she just waved them off and turned to see Bob, coming down the gangway with an expression of knowing sympathy. No one had asked him for selfies today.

"Hey," he said once he was close enough to speak to her softly. "I've been in this business long enough to know some days are just like that. But you know what good thing all those bad days have in common?"

"What?" Natalie asked, so quiet she could barely hear herself.

"Dinner," Diver Bob beamed. "Come on. Let's go home."

And while the thought of Friday night dinner with her mom and stepdad did bring Natalie some relief, it wasn't the true reason she had started to feel better by the time they reached the Perkins Cove parking lot.

The true reason was the fire of purpose, which had started to burn inside her several minutes ago and was now raging with such intensity that she could hardly feel the cold rain spattering on her disposable poncho.

The fire had been sparked by one thing, and one thing only. The thing that had started all these problems. The thing Natalie had decided was to blame for her inability to keep all her plates spinning in the air like the cool, collected girl she so desperately wanted to be.

She was going to find out who Adam Wilson was, and what he wanted. And she was going to expose him to the whole town for the mean, weird jerk he was.

And then—*then*—everything was going to finally, *really* be fine.

CHAPTER TWELVE
Lars

Dogs love to swim.

But they hate baths.

No one knows exactly why.

Well, no *human* does.

Lars, wet and miserable, had a few good ideas.

Swimming was a celebration, something you did when you could, *because* you could. Baths, on the other paw, were something that happened to you whether you wanted it or not. And when they did happen, they came with a sense of judgment: *You have grown dirty. You must be cleansed.* Dogs hated to think they had done something wrong, especially if the response involved a cold shower hose.

Of course, in this specific case, Lars was more open than usual to cleansing. Being scented by Marina had been a nightmare. Washing off the rotten-fish smell was a joy.

But as far as doing things wrong...

Well, Lars knew he had done some things very, very wrong. Things no bath could undo.

"Look at this poor guy," Bob said, rubbing another round of his homemade baking soda mixture around Lars's neck. "He looks like he feels even worse than you do."

"Tall order," Natalie said, not quite looking up. She'd brought her phone into the bathroom, encased in a plastic bag to prevent stray water damage, and had been typing on it furiously for the past several minutes.

"Of course," Bob said. "You've had a rough day, too. I just think—and maybe I'm reading too much into the puppy dog eyes here—but it looks like he feels really, really guilty about what he did."

Yes. Thank you. You get it! Lars wanted to bark, but he was trying not to bark again for a good long time, with an emphasis on *good. But could you tell Natalie? She seems a bit distracted.*

Natalie was *extremely* distracted. She also had a waterproof notepad next to her, and every few minutes she would stop to take a note or cross something out.

"What are you looking for, anyway?" Bob asked.

"Adam Wilson." Natalie growled his name the way Lars might growl Marina's, given the chance. "But he's impossible to find online. And it's such a common name. I mean, *Adam Wilson*. Who's named that?"

"Many people, it sounds like!" Bob joked.

"Yes," Natalie said, completely serious.

Bob seemed unsure about how to respond. He exhaled with relief when Natalie's mother entered the room, knocking lightly on the doorframe as she did so.

"How's the stink squad?" she asked, flashing a sympathetic smile in Lars's direction.

Smiles are cheap, Lars thought wetly. *Try freeing me from this torment. Then maybe we can smile.*

"Whoa, that is a *sad* dog," Mrs. Dugnutt said, so at least Lars was getting his point across. Meanwhile, a tingling sensation was building up in his soaked-through bones. He was gonna . . . he was gonna . . .

"Natalie, why aren't you helping?" Maria pressed. "And why put your phone in a bag if you're not even close enough to the tub to get wet?"

Still typing with her right hand, Natalie held up her left pointer finger as a signal to wait a second.

And in that second, Lars's tingle became an explosion. Before he could stop himself, doggy instinct took over, and he shook his coat out vigorously, like a mop being wrung by a whirlwind. Water and baking soda splashed all over the floors, Maria's socks, every single part of Diver Bob, and the waterproof plastic bag that Natalie had calmly lifted in front of her face at exactly the right moment.

"That's why," said Natalie, and even in his hour of misery, Lars loved how his human knew him better than anyone else. "And I promise to help. Just as soon as I've found what I'm looking for."

"What could you possibly be looking for that can't wait?" Mrs. Dugnutt asked with mild parental exasperation, bending to remove her wet socks.

"Adam Wilson," Natalie said.

"Oh!" Mrs. Dugnutt straightened up, her entire demeanor changing. "Well, in that case, by all means. After what he said about you at the town meeting, I wanted to find that man and—"

Diver Bob's still-dripping eyebrows flashed upward like emergency warning flares, though with Natalie's face buried in her phone, only Lars and Mrs. Dugnutt noticed.

"Wanted to . . . get to know him better," Maria course-corrected sheepishly, remembering to set an example for her daughter. "Because when someone is acting like a jerk, there's probably something going on with them that you don't know about."

"I agree," Natalie said. "That's why I'm trying to dig up his shady history and expose him for a fraud. So I can get to know him better."

Maria shrugged. "Well, can't argue with that logic."

Lars and Diver Bob made hapless, soggy eye contact. The Prater-Dugnutt women were clearly cut from the same cloth. You kind of had to feel sorry for the scissors.

But something Maria had said now bounced around Lars's brain: *When someone is acting like a jerk, there's probably something going on with them you don't know about.*

Lars knew this was correct, because he himself had just acted like a jerk not half an hour ago on the *Searchin' Urchin*. And while Natalie and Bob may have known some of what was going on with Lars—as evidenced by the second round of anti-otter-odor soap that Lars was now being subjected to—it seemed likely that they didn't know all of it.

For example, they might not have known how afraid he was of his friends no longer having time for him. Lars felt like a real dope for barking at Marina the way he had. But when Bangor hadn't shown up to swim today, he'd had a terrible vision of his porpoise pal out playing with Marina, somewhere Lars would never get to join.

Of course, the otter had been alone when they found her, with no Bangor in sight, so it wasn't exactly a rational fear on Lars's part...

But you know what *else* wasn't rational? Getting your weird smell all over poor, innocent, unsuspecting dogs who were just trying to be nice to you! Well, okay, so, dogs actually did that all the time, too, but that was different. That was when they wanted to communicate or mark someone or something they felt protective toward.

Unless... Marina had been doing that to Lars?

Lars felt at the edge of a very big revelation.

So did Natalie, apparently. Maria's words must have gotten through to her, because she had put down her phone long enough to look up at her mother.

"I just hate how he asks me questions like he thinks I'm in over my head," she admitted. "And then, if I don't answer those questions perfectly, everyone else thinks I'm in over my head, too, and then they all think I'm this doofus who needs help."

This seemed to snap Maria out of her own private revenge fantasies.

"Oh, Natalie." She sighed. "You don't *really* feel that way, do you?"

"I don't know." Natalie wrapped her arms around her

knees. "There's just so many people I don't want to let down. You guys. My friends. The Reardons. Dad."

Mrs. Dugnutt slid down until she was next to Natalie on the bathroom floor.

"Those aren't people you need to feel pressured by," Mrs. Dugnutt said, pressing her bare feet against Natalie's stocking feet. "Those are people who love you and want to help you."

"I guess," Natalie said, weighing the idea skeptically in her mind. "But what about everyone who *can't* help me? Bangor, and Marina, and Lars? *They* need *my* help, not the other way around."

"I'm not so sure about that," Bob interjected. "They help you in other ways. The way sea animals help me. They bring you joy. Do you feel like you've been experiencing very much joy recently?"

"A little." Natalie shrugged. "When I make kids laugh on your boat. Or when Lars and I go swimming together."

"Well, isn't it interesting how those moments involve other people being happy, too? I know you made those kids happy, and I bet Lars loves swimming with you."

I do! I do! Your stepdad's a genius! Lars wagged his tail, splashing more water on the genius in question. Bob sputtered and turned off the shower at last, causing Lars to get even more excited—until Bob began the extremely invasive process of squeegeeing the water from Lars's coat with his bare hands.

"It's almost," Bob said, squishing Lars's thigh, "like *you* being happy makes all of *us* who love you happy. It's nice that you want to help all these people, but you have to remember that they'd all love to help you, too, if you ever just ask. What's in your best interest is in our best interest, and seeing you run yourself ragged is in nobody's interest. Seeing you happy is. Do you know why I say 'more makes merry'? Because the more people there are to share your joy with, the bigger that joy can get."

He looked up from where he'd been squelching behind Lars's ears.

"That's how I felt when I got to join your family," he said.

Mrs. Dugnutt beamed at her husband, and Natalie appeared truly caught off guard, looking at her step-father in a way Lars had never seen her do before. She began to lower her phone to the ground.

Then she was struck by a different idea entirely.

"Wait," she said, snapping her phone back up. "*Interests.* Adam keeps saying that he's interested in sea life. It's not much, but it's something. Let me just…"

She returned to typing with a vengeance, muttering as she did so. "Adam Wilson sea life…no…Adam Wilson marine biology…hold on…Adam Wilson aquatic—'"

She stopped.

"Oh wow," she said, apparently having found something. "Oh yes."

And then, as she read further:

"Oh. Oh *no*."

"What is it?" Mrs. Dugnutt asked, craning her neck to see. Lars wanted to get out of the tub and do the same, not least of all because Bob was now reaching for the dreaded hair dryer.

"Call Nancy Jane," Natalie said. "And tell her to call Mayor Maher. Tell *everyone*. Well, almost everyone. We're having an emergency town meeting. Sunday. But this time: *no* outsiders."

She looked up at the adults and Lars, and any anger in her face had been replaced by real, genuine concern.

And what she said next made Lars forget about his bath worries completely:

"Marina and the porpoises are in serious danger."

CHAPTER THIRTEEN
Natalie

Of all the tough jobs Natalie had signed herself up for over the last couple months, few had been more daunting than selling Ogunquit on the idea of a secret town meeting. From her very first phone call with Nancy Jane, Natalie encountered pushback. Nancy Jane's concerns were mainly ethical; she didn't like the idea of sneaking around behind anyone's back. But she could hear the urgency in Natalie's voice, and ultimately she agreed to put the word through to the Mayor.

The rest of the town's concerns had less to do with ethics, and more to do with the fact that the people of Ogunquit had a very shaky grasp on the idea of secrets in general. In Ogunquit, there were only two types of information: old news and exciting new gossip that had yet to make it all the way around town.

What ultimately saved the day for Natalie was that the meeting didn't have to be kept secret from just *anyone* in the town. It was, after all, a *town* meeting, so she wanted lots of people to be there. They just had to keep it secret from Adam Wilson, and anyone he was close to. And since no one could identify a single person he *had* gotten close to, this basically meant the secret was free to be shared with absolutely anyone with the sole exception of Adam. This turned out to be very good for civic engagement, and before long, people weren't just excited to attend the secret meeting; they were suggesting ways to make it even more secret, like holding it after sundown and in a different location than usual. Barnacle Barry, spotting an exciting business opportunity, had offered the after-hours use of his restaurant (plus half-price appetizers). By the end of the weekend, the top-secret town meeting was shaping up to be the see-and-be-seen social event of the season.

And so it was that everyone who was anyone in Ogunquit ended up crammed into the bar and grill section of Barnacle Barry's late that Sunday evening, eagerly watching Natalie and Lars take the stage (which was to say, the raised platform normally reserved for Karaoke Tuesdays). Lars didn't *need* to be onstage with Natalie, but she figured it was safest to keep him close to her side, and far from the side of Barnacle Barry. Barry had been willing to let a dog into his restaurant since the meeting was after hours, but he might have changed his mind if he'd stood close enough to the dog in question to smell that, even two days and several baths later, there was still a slight but undeniable Marina scent lingering faintly around Lars.

Regardless, Lars made for great moral support. Looking out at the packed crowd, Natalie saw everyone from friendly faces (like one Mr. Grundy) to unfriendly faces (the other Mr. Grundy) to every kind of face in between (Nancy Jane, clearly wanting to be supportive but unable to hide a concerned frown).

When had everything gotten so complicated?

Well, one thing was still simple. When she reached down to pet that magic spot just behind Lars's ears, Natalie was swiftly rewarded with the wagging of Lars's tail and a feeling of peace in her heart. She knew her hand would smell all ottery later, but right now, it didn't matter. Maybe Bob had been right: Lars helped just by bringing her joy.

And now it was her turn to help.

With a sudden steeliness that got the crowd's attention better than any gavel, Natalie stood up tall and clicked a remote. Barry's karaoke projector whirred to life, illuminating the screen behind her. Instead of the usual show tune lyrics, though, Natalie was standing in front of a bar graph—the first slide of a presentation she had feverishly prepared over the weekend, working it up between swim practices and sea life tours.

Natalie clicked the remote again, and a long blue bar appeared on the graph.

"Harbor porpoises are like dogs," Natalie said. "And not just because they're both great playmates." She had decided not to waste time introducing herself. The audience already hung on her every word. "They also have similar life spans. A harbor porpoise in the wild has an average life span of about ten years. But in certain cases—if the conditions are right—some have been known to live as long as *twenty* years. Like some dogs."

She smiled down at Lars, who looked up at her and wagged again.

"They should all be so lucky," she said.

Then her smile faded, and she gave the remote another click. A red bar appeared on the graph. It was much, much shorter than the blue bar.

"The average life span of a porpoise in captivity," she continued, "is a few *months.*"

This got the first murmur of the evening. Having

had years to learn from Mayor Maher's mistakes, Natalie moved straight on to the next slide before anyone could speak up and derail her. The next slide was a video: a baby otter being handed over by a ruddy-cheeked middle-aged man in a bright green polo shirt. He gave the otter pup to an excited child, who attempted to hug it and then cried out in dismay when it swiped at his face and squirmed away.

"Otters have similar lifespans, too," said Natalie, "and they're also just as playful. But while they can live well in captivity, they can easily become stressed or frightened if they're not taken care of well. Like, say, for example, if they're passed around a group of strange humans by poorly trained staff at a poorly run park. A poorly run park like this one."

She clicked the remote again. The screen was filled with a logo in the same eye-searing green as the polo worn by the man in the video—the same man who had shabbily photoshopped himself into the logo, waving from between words. The words read AQUATIC AL'S AMAZING ANIMALS. Below, in smaller text, was an address for a highway exit in Deltona, Florida.

Natalie had had a good run, but it was at this point that the natural order of Ogunquit reasserted itself.

"With all due respect," Mr. Reardon spoke up, "why are we talking about some tourist trap in Florida?"

This was exactly what Natalie had hoped someone would ask.

"Because up until a few months ago," she said, "*this* man was employed as their on-site marine biologist and animal trainer."

Click.

The crowd gasped.

Behind Natalie was a corporate headshot of Adam Wilson, wearing a bright green Aquatic Al's polo and attempting something that must, in Adam's mind, have felt like a smile.

"Aquatic Al's is an unaccredited roadside aquarium," Natalie explained. "*Unaccredited* means the international Association of Zoos and Aquariums thought this place was unsafe for animals and wouldn't endorse it. And no wonder. If you search for *Aquatic Al's*, you find all kinds of articles about the shady stuff they've been caught doing, like mishandling that baby otter, or this recent news story"—headlines appeared behind her as she spoke—"where a tip from an anonymous concerned citizen led authorities to discover dolphins and other animals being kept in tanks that were too small for them. Other animals including porpoises."

She would have loved to pause to let this sink in, but there wasn't time. She pressed forward:

"Shortly after that report came out, Aquatic Al's was shut down. Adam left in search of a new job—and a new home. And it turns out, if you ask nicely at the town courthouse, you can find the new address of Ogunquit's latest citizen: Adam Wilson."

"You can do *what*?!" Sammy Reardon squawked.

"Sammy, haven't you ever heard of a phone book?" Mrs. Reardon asked.

"No."

"He makes a point, though," said Mayor Maher. "Isn't this all a bit invasive?"

But he was startled into silence by the next slide—a picture of the new address in question. Adam's new home had a shape like two buildings smashed together. The first building, closest to the camera, was a small wooden shack. There were countless others just like it all around Ogunquit. Except this one had one big thing setting it apart: The second building, which grew around it, flaring out behind the shack like the shell of a hermit crab. It was made out of metal and glass and looked to be twice as large as the wooden house in front of it. The whole frankenbuilding jutted out onto the beach shore behind it, framed on both sides by ocean waves.

"Isn't that—" Mrs. Reardon began.

"Tuna Tim's Tide Tank," Diver Bob said instantly. "'For Kids Who Want to Touch the Ocean,'" he added, recalling Tuna Tim's trademark catchphrase.

"That's up on the north edge of town, right? Didn't they close down last year?" Saul Grundy winked at Bob knowingly. "Bet you must have been pretty happy, Bob. I know he was your main competition for customers around here."

"Oh, the more people teaching kids about the ocean, the better," Diver Bob said earnestly, but then his face darkened. "I will say, though, that some people aren't in it for the right reasons. *Some* people will keep their animals in the wrong kind of tank just because it's cheaper. They put their money before their morays."

A thoughtful silence fell over the crowd.

"Right," Natalie said. "So—"

"I mean, tuna isn't even *really* a tidal fish."

"*Thank you*, Diver Bo—Bob," Natalie said. "And, yes, this place *did* belong to Tuna Ti—to Tim. Now, though, it belongs to Adam Wilson. And you're absolutely right. Some people *do* cut corners when it comes to caring for animals. And if *you* care about animals, those people should make you very uncomfortable."

She took a deep breath. This was the crucial moment.

"Well, from the first day he got here, Adam Wilson made *me* uncomfortable. Since he first showed up on our Sea Life Tours, he's been private and standoffish. Nobody knew where he came from, or what he wanted. He just kept asking all these weird, specific questions—first about where Bangor and the porpoises lived, and then how to find them, and even how to train them. And then Marina showed up, and he started asking the same questions about her. Now we know where he came from—a small, sloppily run aquarium. And we know that right after it got shut down, right when Bangor and the pod were all over the internet, he started making plans to move here and buy *another* small, sloppily run aquarium. And when you know all that … I think it's pretty easy to guess what he wants."

"Natalie," Mayor Maher said, "are you saying what I think you're saying?"

"I imagine I am." Natalie tried to keep the quake of

fear out of her voice. "Adam Wilson wants to find Bangor. He wants to find Bristol, and Belfast, and Kittery, and York. He even wants to find Marina. And once he does, I'd bet you anything he wants to put them all in some tiny tank, just like he helped do to those animals in Florida, so he can keep them all in captivity. And that won't just be *uncomfortable* for those animals." She looked Mayor Maher right in the eye. "That'll be deadly."

The mayor was speechless.

The town was not.

"How do we stop him?" asked someone near the salad bar.

"How could he even pull it *off*? You can't just fish a porpoise out of the water with a butterfly net."

"That's *literally* what a fish net is."

"Oh. Right."

"The porpoises are protected by law—he wouldn't dare."

"Wouldn't he, though? He's clearly done it before."

"Well, yeah, but would he be foolish enough to do it again?"

"It doesn't really matter for the otter." This was Mr. Reardon, who had been processing this news as seriously as he processed everything else. "It's like we said last week—they're not protected by the same laws as harbor porpoises. If he wanted her, he could have her."

This was the conclusion Natalie had come to as well. On some level, hearing another adult say it out loud felt good, because it was nice to know she wasn't overreacting.

On the other hand, it made the danger feel very real.

"So it's settled," Natalie said. "We have to do something."

And then things got *really* real.

"What in the *world* do you think you're going to do?"

Natalie squinted through the bright light of the projector.

And there, stepping out from the shadow of the lobster tank, was Adam Wilson.

In a second, half of Ogunquit was up on its feet. A second later, so was the other half, in a determined effort not to be cheated of a good view.

"You're not supposed to be here," said Mr. Grundy, his arms crossed. "Who invited you?"

"I did."

Heads whipped around, including Natalie's and Lars's, searching to find who had spoken.

They found Nancy Jane.

"I'm sorry, Natalie," she said. "I just didn't feel right plotting behind someone's back—even someone I don't know very well. Ogunquit should be welcoming to all newcomers."

"Even if those newcomers want to hurt defenseless animals?!" Natalie cried. If there was anyone in town she trusted to have her best interests at heart, it was Nancy Jane. Now, though, Natalie's heart felt like it just might break.

"Hurting defenseless animals, huh?" Adam scoffed. "You're one to talk."

Everyone gasped.

"No, I'm serious." Adam took advantage of all eyes swiveling back to him to address the room: "Do you know how dangerous it is to have not one, not two, but *five* harbor porpoises swimming around an active commercial waterway?"

"Look, buddy—" Mr. Prater said, storming out into the aisle, and Natalie felt her blood run hot and cold at the same time.

"Don't *help* me, Dad!" she cried out before she could

166

stop herself. Mr. Prater froze the moment he heard his daughter's voice, which was a relief; she didn't want him making a scene. But when he turned to her and she saw how quietly sad his face was, it felt worse than any commotion ever could.

Not wanting to live with that hurt for a second longer than she had to, Natalie turned back to Adam. "All the commercial boats here use—"

"I've heard you use pingers. Great. That's a good start." Adam took his glasses off and rubbed at his nose. He seemed to be sincerely irritated, like everyone had somehow let him down. "But what about boats just passing through town, who don't know about the local situation? And what if any members of the pod have a baby? Porpoise calves don't hear pingers as well as adult porpoises. Perkins Cove is one big accident just waiting to happen. And now, with this otter renewing press and tourist attention, you're all just throwing fuel on the fire."

"Those porpoises *choose* to come to the harbor," Bob pointed out with trademark calm. "It's in the name, after all. We just do our best to be accommodating."

"Oh, please. You're just as bad as the girl," Adam said, bringing about a new crop of mutters and gasps.

"You've been socializing them to depend on you. Each fish you throw from that absurd boat of yours just encourages the porpoises to depend on humans. But they're still wild, naturally shy animals caught between two worlds."

Natalie couldn't believe what she was hearing. Even worse, she couldn't believe that Adam was actually sort of making sense. So she retreated to a much simpler feeling—outrage.

"And you think the solution is taking them out of the wild to suffer in captivity?" she shot back.

Adam just rolled his eyes as if she was being hopelessly naive. "I never said that! But apparently, everyone here is willing to form an angry mob about it anyway!"

Adam threw his arms in the air, looking, for a brief and ludicrous moment, like one of the lobsters in the tank behind him.

"What is *wrong* with this town?" he asked. "You think *I'm* private and standoffish? You're all *judgmental* and standoffish! You think *I* want to exploit animals for money?"

Adam jabbed a finger at a chalkboard above the bar, where at some point Barnacle Barry had written the words:

BANGORS & MASH: SEA SAUSAGE & PORPOISE
POTATOES FOR JUST $9.99*
*(NOT ACTUALLY PORPOISE.)

"You already are!" Adam cried.

He glared at the room, daring anyone to challenge him. But this time, it wasn't just the mayor who was speechless. It was everyone.

Including Natalie.

Seemingly as disgusted by their silence as he was by their speaking up, Adam huffed, spun around on his heel, and headed for the front door. He slammed through it, disappearing into the night.

An entire town watched him go.

Then an entire town looked back at Natalie.

Nancy Jane looked at her. Her father looked at her. Her mother and her stepdad both looked at her. Each of them looked like they wanted to say something that would help make everything better.

But they all stayed silent.

Probably because moments ago, when one of them had tried to speak up to help her, she had begged them to stay quiet.

Which was funny. Because now, finally, Natalie

felt like she would have done anything for someone to help her.

Anything but ask.

Before she knew what she was doing, Natalie bolted for the back of the building, away from the expectant eyes of Ogunquit, bursting through the back door out onto the patio overlooking Perkins Cove, where the black night bled into the water. It was exactly what Adam Wilson had done moments ago, but in the opposite direction.

Before the door closed behind her, she heard a scrabbling of claws on wood—the sound of Lars following right at her side.

The sound of the one simple, good thing in her life.

A life that had just become really, *truly* complicated.

CHAPTER FOURTEEN
Bangor

By some counts, the Atlantic Ocean contains 85,000,000 cubic miles of water. Within that water are at least 17,500 different species of animals, with each of those species containing countless members.

Bangor did not know these numbers precisely, but he knew his home was large, and that there were many, many fish and other fauna in it (though usually slightly fewer than average in the cubic miles closest to Uncle York).

In short, Bangor knew he could not have been the *only* living soul in the Atlantic Ocean.

But it sure was starting to feel that way.

The sun had only just set when Bangor swam, alone, into Perkins Cove. There should have been at least some small amount of boat traffic, some deep-sea fishing boat making a late return from a day spent out beyond the continental shelf. But in the hour since Bangor's arrival, no one had come in or out. It was like the entire town of

Ogunquit had found something fascinating and important to do on land. Something so important that they'd forgotten all about the amazing big blue biome they'd balanced their lives on the edge of, and the friends they had swimming out there, to boot.

And yet Bangor couldn't shake the odd feeling that the humans he was looking for were somewhere close by—around, but just out of sight.

Well, you could be awfully close to someone and still feel very far away. After the past few days, Bangor knew that better than anyone. In the wake of his big blow-out fight with his mother on Friday, he'd been trying to give the pod a healthy distance while making sure he wasn't *so* distant that Kittery thought he was trying to escape again.

This was a tough balance to strike.

Bangor knew he should have apologized to his mother and told her how much she meant to him. York, who had many years' worth of wisdom under his melon, surely would have called it a great personal victory for Bangor if he did so. But Bangor, who possessed far fewer years and a lot more frustration, couldn't help but feel that rolling over like that would be some sort of defeat. Anyway, Kittery didn't seem interested in hearing much of anything from him right now—just keeping a watchful eye on him. So he stuck around reluctantly, making sure he was seen but not heard.

If this was a tense situation for Bangor and Kittery, poor Bristol seemed to be suffering from it even more. After just a couple days of silence, Bristol burst out in a frenzy of clicking and tail thrashing.

Why can't you two just make up?! If you keep being this quiet, I'm going to run away myself!

Which was, of course, exactly the wrong thing to say to Kittery. She'd become upset, and the pod's already-shaky peace had fallen apart faster than a ship hitting an iceberg. This was when Kittery absolutely forbade anyone from even going near Perkins Cove.

This was also, of course, exactly when Bangor had set off for Perkins Cove.

So now he'd arrived, and even though there was no one to play with and nothing really to do, lingering here still felt easier than going back out to Bibb Rock.

It was actually kind of nice. The boats rocked gently back and forth on waves pulled by the bright moon above. It had been a long time since Bangor had experienced this kind of total peace. It was, in its own small way, an adventure.

Was this, in fact, what it meant to have adventures? To ultimately end up alone? Was there no way to strike out on your own without losing the love and guidance of your family? Was Bangor destined to spend his nights with only the company of the moonlight and the tiny baby mackerel flitting under the dock?

Surely not, right? After all, the first big adventure he'd ever taken had introduced him to his best friend, Lars.

But now, not even Lars was in sight—Lars, who sometimes trotted to the beach on his own when all the humans were off doing whatever boring things they chose to do five days a week. Even the harbormaster's house appeared to be empty, its lights off for the night.

This last part made Bangor a little nervous. He had watched the comings and goings of Perkins Cove long enough to know the harbormaster was responsible for monitoring who came in or out, raising and lowering the drawbridge whenever it was called for, and giving everyone plenty of warning that a boat was on the move.

But there was no sense worrying about it. In addition to echolocation, Bangor had the gift of excellent night vision, all the better for seeing under dark and murky water. He'd notice anything coming toward him. As long as it didn't sneak up from behind him. Which, given how little space the small cove allowed for sneaky maneuvering, should be impossible—

Something rammed into Bangor from behind.

Bangor squealed in fright.

So did the thing that had run into him.

Whirling around, Bangor saw Marina, eyes wide, scrabbling backward through the water by frantically wiggling and splashing her webbed paws. Clearly she had seen Bangor floating alone in the moonlight and decided to surprise him as a fun prank—except she'd done too good a job of surprising him.

(Porpoises, it is worth mentioning, do *not* have excellent senses of smell.)

After a moment's confusion, though, both animals realized their mistake—and Bangor began to laugh. Porpoise laughter, which consists of a quick short shock of pulses that melt into a happy whistle, is one of nature's most remarkable sounds. Within seconds of hearing it, Marina had thrown back her head and began to release a chuckling noise that was, Bangor was willing to bet, the otter equivalent of laughter.

After that, it was game on.

With the entire empty cove at their disposal, Bangor and Marina were able to whip and whizz through the water fearlessly, dodging between boats and breakers. Whenever Marina surfaced, starlight danced in the drops that slid down her whiskers.

If adventuring meant leaving his family, Bangor thought, then maybe he'd just have to buck up and do it. He'd done it before, after all, back on that first fateful, stormy night. That had been an accident, sure, but look what it had brought him: unforgettable friends like Lars, Natalie, and now, Marina. If his family didn't like it, well, they didn't have to follow him around all the time, hassling him and calling after him!

Bangor!

Right, just like that.

Bangor, over here!

Wait. That was actually happening. Someone was clicking to get his attention.

Bangor froze, and Marina shot past him, nearly slamming into the Grundy family boat, the *Kelly Natasha*. After she had stopped herself, Marina turned and followed Bangor's gaze to see who had joined them.

There, joyfully racing toward them, was . . .

Bristol?! Bangor squeaked in shock. *What are you doing here?! Mom told you not to come here! She's going to blow her top! More than usual!*

For a moment, Bristol slowed down, her whistle descending in pitch. *Yeah, I know. It makes me sad.* Then she brightened up again and swam circles around her older brother. *But I'm* tired *of being sad! I* miss *you! Let's run away! I don't care if it means never seeing them again—I want to be like* you*!*

At first, this made Bangor's heart pound with joy. Hearing that his little sister loved him so much that she'd follow him to the ends of the ocean … it was every big brother's dream.

At the same time, though …

Let's run away!

It was exactly the sentiment Bangor had been thinking to himself only moments ago. But now, hearing Bristol express it, swearing she never needed to see her family again, it sounded … childish.

Of course, his family didn't just follow him around. They supported him. They brought him joy. Look how much joy he'd felt just from seeing Bristol's smiling snout right now, for instance.

Suddenly with a clarity as silver and pure as the

moon on the water, Bangor understood that he had to set things right with his mother.

Which probably started with him and his little sister returning to the pod.

Bristol, I—

But Bangor didn't get very far as the world exploded in bubbles and squeaking. Marina had been looking curiously back and forth as the two porpoises argued in a language she could not understand, and now she had chosen to make it clear that there had been entirely too much clicking around here and not nearly enough playing.

Bristol seemed to agree, instantly whistling with excitement and executing a barrel roll as Marina blazed past her. As the otter curved tightly to make her return and Bristol spun around to face her, Bangor realized that his sister and Marina had never really gotten the chance to play together one-on-one. And Marina was quick to catch on to the advantages of having such a small playmate. Just when it seemed she was about to rocket straight into Bristol's snout, Marina suddenly shot upward and out of the water, where she flew, tip to tail, *lengthwise* over Bristol's entire body, splashing back into the water behind the young porpoise as Bristol laughed in amazement.

Okay, Bangor thought, laughing as well despite himself. *Maybe going home can wait just a bit.*

Then Marina darted off behind a boat, and Bristol shot forward to find her, followed bemusedly by Bangor.

The trio played together like this for the next several minutes. If anyone had been around to see it, they would have been amazed at the sight of the two porpoises and the otter rejoicing under the starry night sky, communicating with one another in a way that went deeper than any language. Bangor never wanted it to end.

But he knew that it had to eventually. And he especially knew it when, after taking a quick break to huff and puff and catch her breath, Bristol raced out in the direction of the drawbridge. She looked out at the wide dark ocean beyond, where shadows and light moved like an invitation, and then turned back to her older brother to ask, *Can we do this every day when we've run away together?*

Okay. That was his cue.

Bristol, Bangor said, drifting gently toward his sister. *We can't run away together. We—*

And then he realized: One of those shadows out there wasn't just a shadow.

It wasn't a big boat; not a fisherman's boat like *The Marina*, or a modified yacht like the *Searchin' Urchin*. It was a motorboat, small enough to pass beneath the drawbridge with no problem. And it didn't have any pingers on, indicating that it wasn't from around here—just some tourists, probably out for a late-night pleasure cruise. It was possible they didn't know which cove they were pulling into, or even which town.

That wasn't the only thing they didn't know. Porpoises may have had excellent night vision, but humans... not so much. Bangor had watched enough boats bump clumsily into docks after sunset to know that human vision got *way* worse out on the water at night. To them, the gray flash of a porpoise flank in the dark might as well have been just another line of moonlight on the water.

Bangor, though, could see it all too perfectly as the boat bore down on his baby sister.

It wasn't a big boat.

But Bristol wasn't a big porpoise.

And because she was looking straight at her older brother, she had no clue what was coming for her. If she turned now, the boat would only confuse her echolocation. This was it. This was what Kittery had warned her children about. Her worst nightmare. *Bangor's* worst nightmare: A boat was going to hit his little sister. Nothing short of a miracle could stop it.

Bangor would just have to be a miracle.

He raced forward, faster than he'd ever known he could. He experienced the following things in rapid succession:

A squeak of surprise from Bristol.

A cry of confusion from the humans in the boat as they finally saw something moving in the black waves below.

A *thud* as Bangor smashed into his sister, sending her reeling through the water, out of the path of the boat.

A red dull bloom of pain in Bangor's mind, and the sluggish, confused thought: *Hitting Bristol shouldn't have hurt that much, right? She's not that big. So why does it feel like I ... just ... hit ... something much bigger ...*

It was funny. Hypothetically this was the most pain Bangor had ever felt in his life. But as he drifted through the water in a daze, he found so many other things to focus on instead:

The cold, smooth surface of the rocky shore as he washed up against it and stayed there, suddenly too tired to swim.

The roar of the boat's motor as it peeled out of the cove, headed who knew where—just anywhere away from here.

Bristol poking her head out of the water inches from where Bangor was beached on the shore, whistling frantically, *Get up! Get up! Bangor, you have to get up!*

Bangor tried and failed to say something in response.

I'm going to get Mom! I'm going to get everyone! You just … stay here!

And then Bristol was tearing out of the cove, too, back out into the ocean.

And Bangor was alone.

Well, not quite alone. Marina raced up onto the rocks around him, sniffing and squeaking. She leaned forward, got something on her whiskers, and jerked back as if she'd been shocked by electricity. She cleaned it off and scampered up to Bangor's melon, chittering and chattering in his ear, but he was as helpless to respond to her as he'd been with his sister.

Well, it was nice to have some company, at least.

Then Marina looked up at the lights of Ogunquit. She twitched her nose as if smelling something familiar.

Then she tore off toward land, disappearing into the night.

Classic Marina, Bangor thought weakly.

Well, no matter. Before, Bangor had felt like the only living soul in the ocean. Now he got to feel like the only living soul on land, too. It was kind of impressive in a delirious sort of way.

With a huff that should have been a laugh, Bangor had the same thought he had just a short while ago:

Where is *everyone?*

CHAPTER FIFTEEN
Lars

There was a new smell on the night air. Something rusty and odd that Lars had never smelled before.

He didn't like it.

But right now, his attention was reserved for a smell he disliked even more—the smell coming off Natalie. Not that she smelled bad—to Lars's nostrils, Natalie could never smell bad. But she smelled *sad*. Shame and regret spilled off her in waves.

They were out behind Barnacle Barry's dockside patio, hiding on a set of steps that led down to the water. Natalie was shivering into her windbreaker, and Lars had pressed himself up against her to share some of his body heat, even though he could *also* smell some fries a few feet away that some clumsy customer had dropped between the slats of the wooden patio. From the warmth of the scent, they were only a few hours old, perfectly good to eat.

But some things were even more important than fries.

Things like his human, who had been stretching herself thin for weeks now, and had finally come undone.

"I mean, was he *right?* He was kind of right...right?" Natalie had been talking half to herself, half to Lars, for a few minutes now, gasping the questions out between sniffles. "But he didn't *deny* anything I said about him. So I *think* I was right. Right? But the things he said about Bangor, and the town...*those* weren't all wrong. So was *I* wrong?"

No! Lars wanted to bark. *You could never be wrong! Anyone who makes you upset is obviously in the wrong and, also, is a jerk!*

But somehow, this did not seem like what Natalie needed to hear right now.

After one more big shuddering gasp, Natalie wiped her nose with her windbreaker sleeve and forced herself to slowly exhale. Then she hugged Lars close to her, a sweet moment only slightly marred by her rubbing her windbreaker sleeve off on Lars's fur. Lars didn't mind, though. What else were friends for?

"He was right about one thing," Natalie admitted quietly, once her breathing was back under control. "I *have* been judgy and standoffish. And not just to him. Every time Dad has wanted to help me, or the twins, or anyone else…I shut them out. Maybe I need to stop doing that. Maybe Bob was right. If I *really* want to do right by everyone, maybe I need to start by talking to them about how I'm actually feeling."

She gazed down the steps and into the cold water, which lapped patiently against the rocky sand beneath the docks.

"And maybe that even includes Adam Wilson," she said at last. "Maybe if I'd talked to him directly, I could have avoided embarrassing us both in front of everyone."

This seemed like a pretty big ask to Lars. Adam was the one who'd been rude to Natalie. Why should *she* have to reach out to *him* first?

But then he thought about Marina, and how rude she'd been to *him*.

He'd been turning the pieces over in his mind all weekend. The loneliness of Marina's single-otter den. The sneaking suspicion that she had scented Lars *not* to mock him but to claim him as a possible friend. Or even…a possible family member. If his time with Natalie and Bangor had taught Lars anything, it was that family could come from anywhere if you only knew where to look.

Had Marina been reaching out to him, and he'd ignored it? Was Marina his Adam Wilson—someone he'd misjudged? Should he give her a second chance? When it came right down to it, *could* he?

Well, he'd get a chance to find out very soon.

Because now his nose twitched at the arrival of a familiar fishy scent, and not one second later, Marina had popped her furry little head over the edge of the patio to stare straight down at Natalie and Lars.

"Ohmigosh!" Natalie gasped, jumping so sharply in surprise that she accidentally pushed Lars off the steps and onto the gravelly beach below. "Oh, sorry, Lars, I just— You came out of *nowhere!*"

Marina chirped something in response and then slid through the posts of the patio railing and skittered down the stairs in a movement so fluid it was like watching a mountain stream with paws. Natalie took a sharp breath and held it as the otter rushed past her, so close that they were separated by mere millimeters. Then Marina was down at the water's edge, where she stopped and turned.

To look directly at Lars.

She's going to scent you, growled a fearful voice from somewhere in the back of Lars's canine brainstem. *She's going to scent you again, and it'll smell even worse than before, and you're just sitting there waiting for it—*

But if Lars was ever going to set a good example for Natalie—for *himself*—now was his moment. No more would he be the barking, *bad* dog who scared away otters and ruined Natalie's sea life tours and felt guilty and gross in bathtubs afterward. He was a new Lars, a Lars who let people into his heart, who understood that when people acted like jerks, there was usually something going on with them that you didn't know about.

Of course, it was *very* hard to know what was going on with Marina. Who, this whole time, had just kept staring at Lars.

And then she jumped at him.

It was just a play jump, or at least Lars thought it was—it didn't take her far enough to crash into him, and dog only knew that Marina was fast enough to have done that if she'd wanted to. Lars reared back a little in surprise, but he didn't snap or run. Marina darted a little way down the beach and then stopped, looking back as if expecting Lars to chase after her.

But Lars just stayed exactly where he was and wagged his tail, trying to be the bigger mammal. *Do you want to play? Is that what this is? You can just ask. I mean you can't, like,* actually *ask, but you don't have to be* rude.

In response, Marina ran back toward him ... stopped inches away from Lars's face ... and then spun around in a cyclone of fur, whipping Lars's nose with her tail in the process, leaving him cross-eyed and dazed.

Natalie cried out, clearly stifling a laugh. "Is this ... what are you doing? Lars, are you okay?"

But Lars was determined to prove he'd be alright, even as Marina scampered off again, back in the same direction. If he didn't know better, he'd have thought Marina *wanted* him to chase her. Well, too bad, otter. This dog had turned over a new leaf.

Marina, seeing that she was getting no response, grumbled in what appeared for all the world to be a squeaky little show of impatience.

Then she ran back again—not toward Lars this time, but into the darkness under Barnacle Barry's dock, vanishing instantly as her brown fur blended into the shadows beneath the patio.

Lars and Natalie both stared into the patch of darkness where the otter had gone.

"Is she—" Natalie began.

And then Lars, whose nose had just begun to recover from its drubbing, was hit *again.*

By a French fry.

As in, physically hit.

As if someone had picked up one of Lars's precious spilled French fries and then thrown them from under the dock.

Oh, that was *it*.

Teasing, Lars could handle. Bad scents? Those could be washed off.

But the flaunting of opposable thumbs?

That was *unforgivable*.

In an instant, Lars was tearing after Marina's all-too-followable scent, yowling and growling his head off. He was, quite literally, barking mad.

"Lars, *no*! Not *again*!" Natalie cried. But she was helpless to follow Lars under the darkness of the dock.

Not for long, though—because Marina had curved around within seconds, leading Lars right back out from under the patio and up along the shore, heading in the direction she had tried to run twice now already. Natalie, seeing the two animals streak out from the shadows, leaped from the steps onto the beach and took off after them.

Marina was, infuriatingly, even faster on land than she was on water—but Lars was pretty darn fast himself, and if Natalie had proved one thing over the past couple years, it was her ability to keep up with Lars when she really had to. Like some kind of bizarre late-night running club, the three of them tore over the bumps and boulders that made up so much of the Maine coastline, with Natalie shouting, Lars barking, and Marina chirruping the whole way. Clumps of seabirds scattered into the air, and lights flicked on in the backs of seaside properties, but nothing distracted Marina, and thus, nothing distracted Lars.

Well, one thing was starting to. The farther they ran up the side of Perkins Cove, the more Lars began to notice that strange new smell he'd detected earlier—a smell of sadness and ... pain?

Lars tried to shake it off, but the smell was only getting stronger, almost as if they were running straight toward it. Before Lars could pursue this thought further, though, Marina arrived at a particularly large boulder and leaped over it, disappearing behind its bulk. Then she poked her head back above it, looking back at them pleadingly.

Lars skidded to a halt on the salty rocks.

A few seconds later, Natalie pulled up behind him,

taking a deep breath to give him the scolding of a lifetime.

Then she saw what Lars was looking at.

And that breath turned into a wail of shock and horror.

Because Marina hadn't jumped over a large boulder.

She'd jumped over Bangor, who was beached on the shore.

CHAPTER SIXTEEN
Natalie

Perkins Cove is one big accident just waiting to happen.

Adam Wilson's words had scared Natalie because she had feared that they might be true. Well, those words weren't true anymore.

Because the accident had already happened.

Funny how it didn't help with the fear.

Bangor lay on his side, a red blotch running down his flank. The tide worried his tail, but it was swiftly receding, leaving Bangor high, dry, and helpless.

Natalie had done a lot of research about harbor porpoises over the last couple years. You couldn't do that without occasionally reading about beached or stranded porpoises. At the time, Natalie had glossed hurriedly over the information as if walking past a graveyard, hoping it was something she would never have to use. Now, the few facts she'd retained flashed out of her mind like ghosts rising from that graveyard:

First and foremost: Do not touch the stranded animal—

Not the animal, she thought desperately. This was her friend—*Bangor*—

Okay. Do not touch Bangor without a professional around to help.

Second: Find out if he's even still alive.

You were supposed to do this by checking to see if the—if *he*—was still breathing.

The problem with porpoises was that they breathed only very rarely.

As Natalie waited and watched Bangor's blowhole for signs of motion, she found she was holding her own breath. She didn't know for how long. It could have been one minute. It could have been six. She'd already felt like she was about to pass out before she'd taken the breath, so it really didn't make much difference.

Then, just when Natalie felt like she was going to collapse into herself:

Puff.

The sound was weak and heartbreaking, but unde-niable. Bangor had exhaled. He was breathing. And therefore, so was Natalie.

Right. So. A professional. What was she going to do? She had to find someone. She had to . . .

For a brief and shameful moment, Natalie felt a stab

of fear at the thought of telling someone what had happened to Bangor. The fear said: *If you go tell someone a boat ran into Bangor, they'll all know Adam was right. You're going to feel so embarrassed.*

But now, Natalie recognized that voice for what it was: pride. And pride had kept her isolated for too long. It had almost ruined her life. She wouldn't let it ruin anyone else's.

Especially not Bangor's.

She needed to ask for help.

"Come on, Lars," Natalie said, and when Lars looked up at her, her heart broke all over again—she'd never seen her little stray dog look so lost. Well, she felt lost, too, but right now, she knew exactly where they needed to go.

"Come on, boy," she repeated, walking backward just long enough to make sure that Lars was following her. Once he started trotting after her, she picked up the pace, and then turned and ran.

As she hurried back the way they'd come, her mind raced as fast as her feet. Who would be most helpful right now? Mayor Maher, with all his town resources? Her dad, who she knew would leap into helping her, no questions asked? Diver Bob, who knew so much about sea life? Come to think of it, when it came to knowledge of sea life—what about . . . Adam Wilson? She didn't like that idea at all, for multiple reasons, but maybe it was worth holding on to as a last resort.

As she stormed up the steps of Barry's back patio, racing across the wooden boards and around the side of the restaurant to the Perkins Cove parking lot out front, she was feeling pretty good about the chain of command she'd come up with. First her dad. Then Bob. Then the mayor. *Then*, if all else failed, Adam Wilson.

Then she got to the parking lot and found all four of them at once.

Plus Nancy Jane.

And her mother.

Who was *shaking Adam Wilson's hand*.

What?!

"What are you all *doing* here?" Natalie blurted out, unable to stop herself.

The adults whipped around, startled by her sudden entrance.

"Natalie!" Her dad stepped toward her, freezing when he saw how shaken she was. "Are you okay? I would have gone after you, but I figured you wanted some space, and—"

"No, Dad," Natalie said, her words tumbling out as fast as his. "I'm so sorry I made you feel that way, that's—that's not important right now, though."

Just then, Lars appeared behind Natalie, and Nancy Jane, taking the two of them in, noticed how out of breath they both were.

"Natalie?" she asked. "Is everything okay?"

"No," Natalie croaked. "No, it's not okay at all."

She looked from Nancy Jane to her dad to Diver Bob. With all her might, she tried to avoid the questioning eyes of Mayor Maher and Adam Wilson.

"Bangor's been beached," she said. "I think he got hit by a boat."

The adults were stunned. None of them knew what to say.

Except for one. The one she'd been keeping out of her sight line.

"I can help," said Adam Wilson.

Now, not only did Natalie look at him, she stared at him, wide-eyed and skeptical.

"Okay, seriously," she said. "What *is* your deal?!"

Natalie's mom stepped forward.

"We were just finding that out," she said. "We caught up to him after the meeting ended. It turns out he—"

But Adam just held up a hand, maintaining eye contact with Natalie.

"There's no time for that," he said. "Every second counts right now. Natalie, do you trust that I want what's best for this porpoise?"

Natalie hesitated.

"Look, do you want my help or not?" Adam asked.

Just an hour ago, Natalie's reaction to that question would have been *it's complicated*. But now? Nothing had ever been simpler.

"Of course," she said. "Of course I do. Please. Please help me. Help Bangor."

"Okay," Adam said, backing away from the group while fishing his car keys out of his pocket and pressing them twice. A pickup truck several spots away from them lit up—a truck, Natalie realized, that she had seen before, sitting in various spots around the lot as she'd run to and from work over the past few weeks. She'd noticed it because of the strange apparatus that stuck out of the back—like the kind of rack tourists used to hold kayaks or canoes, but oddly different.

"Did anyone else drive here?" Adam asked, and Mayor Maher raised his hand. "Great. Everyone that can fit, go with him. Mr. Mayor, you follow me."

The adults headed for the mayor's car while Natalie headed for the passenger seat of Adam's truck.

"What are you doing?" asked Adam, Mr. Prater, and Mrs. Dugnutt, all at the same time.

"I'm the only one here who knows where Bangor is," Natalie said. "I'm navigating."

Adam grunted in reluctant acknowledgment. Nancy Jane looked like she wanted to say something, but Mr. Prater put his hand on her arm.

Mr. Prater nodded at Natalie. "Go."

Natalie nodded back and then ran for the passenger seat of Adam Wilson's pickup.

"Seat belt," Adam said as he jammed the key into the ignition.

Once again, Natalie regarded him skeptically. Adam Wilson cared about *her* safety?

"The last thing we need is *another* person getting hurt tonight," Adam said tersely. "It'd be ... inefficient."

Natalie shrugged and pulled the seat belt tight across her lap. Satisfied, Adam grunted again and turned the key. And the two of them drove off, side by side, to save a porpoise.

CHAPTER SEVENTEEN
Bangor

Looking back on his life, Bangor had made quite a few miracles happen in his time.

First there was the time he had met his best friend, when he had swum up at exactly the right moment to save Lars from drowning in a storm.

And again, just now, when he had kept Bristol safe from the boat. That had been a *great* miracle.

Okay, so that was only two examples, but it still felt higher than average. Two miracles in one lifetime? The odds were, frankly, miraculous. And if this was the end, Bangor could go out proud of having done both of those things in his life.

It was just that he'd have preferred not to go out at all. What he'd *really* have preferred was a third miracle. One he didn't have to make happen. One that happened to him.

One may have been happening now. Bangor wasn't sure. All he knew was that being washed up on the shore was less painful than he'd assumed it would be. He'd seen fish do it before, and they always flipped and flopped like they were in agony. But harbor porpoises weren't fish; they were mammals, and Bangor didn't need water to breathe the way fish did. And while he knew he was wounded, something in his brain seemed to be dulling his senses, keeping the ache of the wound to a bare minimum. So he was breathing, and he wasn't in too much pain. That was sort of miraculous.

Though as the tide rolled out, he could feel his skin getting steadily dryer—much dryer than it was ever meant to be. It felt like wearing a scratchy coat, one that steadily got hotter and tighter.

So, maybe not a miracle, then.

He lay there like that for a while, alone, in the dark.

Then a new development put Bangor back on miracle watch: Marina returned, followed almost immediately by Lars and Natalie. This seemed, in fact, *so* miraculous that Bangor hardly dared believe it. Was he hallucinating? He'd daydreamed before, but he'd never had a daydream quite this vivid. Then again, he'd never been out of the water like this, either, so, unexplored territory all around.

He tried to wave his flippers to say hello to his

friends, but by now the itchy coat feeling was so constricting that he could barely move. The most he could manage was a light *puff.* In response, Natalie released an odd, primal, primate noise, halfway between relief and anguish.

No, no, don't be sad, Bangor wanted to click. *I'm fine. I think.*

But try as he might, he just couldn't seem to speak up right now. And then Natalie and Lars were gone again.

So. Two strikes on the miracle front, it would seem.

At this point, Bangor blacked out for a bit. It was an odd experience for a member of a species who had never technically slept before. It was kind of like traveling through time. One second you closed your eyes with waves trickling beneath your tail; the next, you opened them, and the tide was so far out you couldn't feel it anymore. Just that suffocating dryness.

Was *that* a miracle? Time travel? Bangor wasn't sure. It sort of felt like cheating. And it wasn't very fun.

Then he heard a roar in the distance. One that got louder and louder until it was practically deafening.

Suddenly the roar stopped, just when it felt like it

was right on top of him. Then there were footsteps and yelling.

"Hold on, buddy," Bangor heard Natalie say, crouching in front of him. "We're gonna get you out of here."

Lars snuffled up to him as well, giving him a comforting lick and a whine.

Bangor couldn't understand either of them, but the sounds were reassuring. He puffed.

Puffing hurt.

There was no time to focus on that, though. Another human had appeared, squinting at Bangor before straightening up. Then there were a lot of words that Bangor didn't understand, spoken in tight and urgent voices:

"How long has he been out of the water?"

"I don't know, I just—I found him when ... when Marina ... I guess she's not here anymore."

"What are you talking about?"

"Never mind."

"Okay, well—a porpoise can survive several hours on land, as long as he's cool and wet. He's still breathing, and it's definitely cool out here tonight, so that just leaves wet. Our first priority is hydrating him. There are buckets in my truck bed if somebody can start filling them with water from the ocean. Then you're gonna pour that water on him."

"We'll do it." That was a deeper voice—one Bangor recognized as Natalie's father.

"Great. And Ms. Renaud—"

"Please, Adam. Call me Nancy Jane."

"Okay, Nancy Jane. If you could grab some towels to soak, we're gonna lay those on him as well. Actually— let me come with you. There's some other stuff in there we'll need..."

The voices receded, then returned. Someone knelt close to Bangor—*really* close to him, right above his blowhole. With only one eyeball pointing upward, Bangor could roll it around as much as he wanted, but he couldn't see what the newcomer was doing.

"What are you *doing*?"

"I'm checking the blowhole to make sure there's not anything obstructing it—sand or silt or worse. Looks like he's good. So it really is just the dehydration we need to worry about. Speaking of— Ah, thank you, Jim."

"Please, Adam. Call me Mr. Prater."

And with those words came a cooling wave of immense relief: a bucket's worth of cold water being poured, slowly and sweetly, along Bangor's body. As soon as that bucket clattered to the ground, another started pouring in its place. The newcomer who had gotten up in Bangor's personal space now circled around to the other side of him, where he began laying out a big blue tarp he had apparently taken from his truck, lining the waterproof edge up right alongside Bangor's belly.

"Great. Keep that up, and the towels—there we go, Nancy Jane, thank you. Great, we're doing great."

"I'm sorry? What about the *wound*?"

"Okay, yes, that's a concern. But not as much as you'd think. Cetaceans—dolphins, porpoises, whales—they heal remarkably well. Shark bites, propeller blades, you name it. They bounce back faster than a human would, and their blubber contains natural antibiotics that help prevent wound infection. We'll want to halt the bleeding and administer some IV fluids once we've arrived, of course, and take some other steps, but for now if we can just get him onto the tarp—"

"Arrived? Arrived *where*?"

"Less talking, more pushing. Porpoises are heavy. Can someone help?"

A cavalcade of footsteps fell into line behind Bangor in that peripheral zone where he couldn't see. Then several pairs of hands lined up along his back—including a smaller pair near his dorsal fin. That had to be Natalie.

Gently but firmly the hands pushed. For the first time since washing out of the water, Bangor felt himself roll right-side up, his underbelly landing squarely on the blue tarp.

"We did it!"

"Now what?"

"I've got blankets in the truck bed. It should be nice and soft for him. We just have to lift him in there."

"How are we gonna do *that*? This guy's heavy, and . . . don't repeat this to my voters, but my back has been acting up recently."

"Relax. That's what this is for."

From Bangor's new position, he could see something he hadn't before: the car closest to him. It was clearly the truck from which all these materials had been coming, because it had one more big piece of equipment to contribute—a bizarre rack that, when pulled up and out, unfolded to stretch past the truck's back half, dangling a cable with a hook over the ground. With its pulleys and winches, the whole thing looked not unlike the rigs Bangor had seen on the sides of Mr. Prater's boat.

The man who had been doing most of the talking

pulled up the edges of the tarp, looping a long rope through the holes at the tarp's edge. He fastened that rope to the hook at the end of the pulley system, then pulled hard on a cable attached to the truck.

And now Bangor knew he had to be hallucinating.

Because he was starting to fly.

Harbor porpoises have three stomachs, and all three of Bangor's lurched as he pulled up into the air. He'd always felt weightless in the ocean, but this was an entirely new kind of weightlessness, one with no water pressure to moor him—just the dropping away of the world as he rose up and up.

He found himself at eye level with Natalie.

"Hi," she breathed, clearly as stunned as Bangor was.

"Okay. Ji—Mr. Prater, can you help me with this? I've seen you work a pulley before. We just need . . . to . . . lower him . . . gently . . ."

With a few more lurches and swings, Bangor moved forward in a slight descent, eventually touching down on a surprisingly soft surface.

"Is he gonna be okay?"

"Absolutely. I've covered the entire truck bed with blankets. It should be comfortable enough. Though we really should have someone back there to keep him hydrated. But I guess that'd be impossible with the buckets sloshing everywhere—"

"I'll do it." Natalie's voice cut in. "I can wring out more towels on him as we move."

"How would you even fit in there?" That was her father again, sounding concerned.

"Oh, she'd fit in there. I hadn't thought about it, but…" The talkative newcomer seemed to be mulling something over. "I got this truck to hold dolphins, and harbor porpoises are much smaller animals. Look, there's plenty of extra room."

"I'm sorry, you got this truck for *what*?!"

"How many times do I have to say this? We don't have time to quibble. Look, Natalie, you can ride with the porpoise, just…be careful. Now, can we get moving?"

"*Wruff!*"

"Lars wants to go in the truck bed, too. Bangor is his friend."

"I'm sorry. You're telling me we need to listen to a *dog* because he's *friends* with—"

"I thought there was no time for quibbling, Mr. Wilson."

There was a pause.

"Not you, too, Nancy Jane."

"Oh, *especially* me, Adam."

Pause two.

"*Fine.* Every mammal who's getting in the truck bed, get in the truck bed. Everyone else, get back in the mayor's car and follow me. We'll need all those hands again when we get where we're going."

Bangor was facing the inside of the truck bed now, but he could hear footsteps dispersing, even as voices carried:

"Why are you looking at me like that, Mark?"

"You're incredible, Nancy Jane. Do I say that enough?"

"You say it every day."

"That's not enough."

Then a series of *thunks* as each human got into their respective cars.

Each except for one.

As the truck's engine rumbled to life, Natalie clambered up along Bangor's right side, taking care not to bump into his wounded flank. Once the girl had stabilized herself against the corner of the truck bed, she leaned over Bangor, muttering soothing sounds and rubbing his melon comfortingly with one hand while using the other to squeeze salt water from a towel. Each drop that splashed on his back and ran down his side felt like a concentrated burst of kindness.

Meanwhile, on his left, Lars lay down on the blankets next to him. As the truck juddered and turned, heading away from the shore and toward the main road, Lars provided a cushy, furry ballast. More than that, he provided sympathetic eye contact, and the comfort of a good and loyal friend.

And then, just as the truck was about to turn onto the road, there was a soft *thump* from the back of the truck bed, a gasp from Natalie, and a blur of brown movement.

And there, squeezing in between the three souls already present, was Marina.

"Whoa, Marina!" Natalie said. "You're probably not supposed to be in here. Adam is gonna flip. Or Lars will."

The four of them all regarded one another in wary silence. Natalie seemed to be looking meaningfully over Bangor's head at Lars. But Lars just wagged his tail a few times, bumping it lightly against Bangor's left flank, as if silently greeting Marina.

"Or . . . maybe he won't flip," Natalie said eventually. "And maybe Adam doesn't need to know."

Marina chirruped quietly, like she understood the need for stealth. Then she moved forward and gingerly rubbed her soft face against Bangor's melon. Her long whiskers tickled like spindly seaweed, and between that and the restoring effect of the seawater, Bangor almost had enough energy to laugh.

Almost.

He wasn't out of danger yet. He knew that. But as the truck drove on through the darkness, heading goodness only knew where, Bangor felt that maybe he'd gotten his miracle after all. And the miracle wasn't time travel or the ability to fly.

The miracle was a girl, a dog, an otter, and a well-loved porpoise, all traveling together, in hope, and fear, and tender silence, beneath a star-filled sky.

CHAPTER EIGHTEEN
Natalie

Natalie was not surprised when Adam's truck pulled up to Tuna Tim's Tide Tank.

She *was* surprised when she saw how it had changed.

Gone were the flashing neon signs with the business's name and the one below that read PET A SHARK IN OUR SHED PARK! Someone had installed an accessible ramp leading up to the front door. And that same someone had added a few *new* parking spaces—including the one Adam had just pulled into—that butted right up against a side door in the metal-and-glass wing of the building. These new spaces were all labeled RESERVED FOR EMERGENCY PARKING.

What kind of tourist trap needed *emergency* parking?

As Natalie cautiously pulled herself to her feet, Adam shut off the truck and emerged from the driver's seat. A couple of seconds later, the mayor's car pulled up to the side of the building and began to unload as well.

"How's he doing?" Adam asked, gesturing at Bangor.

Natalie turned. Somehow, Marina had already vanished. That was one fast otter.

"He's still breathing," Natalie said, hopping out of the truck and lifting Lars after her. "And I think the water is making a big difference. But his wound—"

"Right." Adam hurried to hitch the tarp back up to the pulley system, tossing Natalie a ring of keys as he did so. "Get the doors. Everyone else, get ready. I can move him out of the truck with this, but from there, we'll need to carry him into the marine mammal tank ourselves."

He pulled, and Bangor started to rise from the truck. Once again, Natalie was struck by the sight of her aquatic friend hovering through the air, gazing down at her from within his tightly wrapped tarp like extremely confused sushi.

This whole situation was entirely weird.

But the weirdest thing of all might have been the feeling Natalie got, as Bangor touched down on the ground and she started to run for the doorway, that her friend might actually get out of this okay.

This, unfortunately, was when the press arrived.

"Hey, I told you they were over here! Look! Look, everyone, they're over here around the side!"

In what was beginning to be a regular occurrence for Natalie, the world was suddenly full of flashing lights and microphones.

"Mr. Wilson! What do you have to say about your past involvement at an unaccredited aquarium?"

"Is it true you intend to illegally capture wild porpoises? Are you— Oh my gosh, are you *abducting one right now?*"

"How fast does news *move* in this town?!" Adam barked. "We'll never get him inside if they keep—"

"I'll hold them off!" Mayor Maher said with all the nobility and conviction of a man who truly does not want to lift a harbor porpoise.

He strode toward the press confidently. Natalie fumbled with the keys, trying one after the other in the lock—that one wasn't right—no, not that one either—while craning her neck to watch.

"And *how* do you plan to distract them?" Nancy Jane was asking, following the mayor, seemingly for her own amusement as much as anything else.

"Oh, I'll think of something."

"Mr. Mayor," said a reporter who Natalie recognized as the woman she'd tricked just a couple weeks ago. "What are you doing here, in the middle of the night, with Adam Wilson and a...purloined porpoise? Do you know about the accusations against him? Adam Wilson, I mean. Not the porpoise."

"You know who knows something about Adam Wilson?" Mayor Maher boomed.

The press fell instantly quiet, in a way that the attendants of an Ogunquit town meeting had never once done.

The mayor beamed like a man who had just discovered he could fly.

"I'll tell you who knows," he said. "Nancy Jane Renaud."

He turned to Nancy Jane, who—after several years spent seeming like she was always one step ahead of the mayor—looked genuinely, delightedly surprised.

"From the moment Adam Wilson came to town, Nancy Jane has been one of the few people to treat him with kindness and empathy—but also courage and grit. I know how amazing that is, because it's how she treats me every day. And it's made me realize I need some courage and grit as well."

"Okay, Mr. Mayor," said the reporter. "But what does this have to do with—"

Mayor Maher turned to Nancy Jane and dropped to one knee.

"Nancy Jane ... I've been as amazed by you tonight as I have been every day I've known you. What's really amazing is that I didn't ask you this sooner. Will you marry me?"

Nancy Jane's words were lost in a storm of camera flashes and gasps, but from her smile and the way the mayor leaped to his feet, it was pretty clear what she'd said.

It was also an incredible distraction. It wasn't what they'd come here for, and it wouldn't hold them for long, but the press knew a great human-interest story when they saw one, and for a moment they clustered around the happy couple, clamoring for a few words from Nancy Jane.

"That's our cue," said Natalie's mother. "Let's go!"

Right as Natalie found the right key, and the door swung open.

The four remaining adults each took a corner of the tarp and strained to lift Bangor into the air, hurrying him forward while they had the strength to carry him. Natalie held the door open, and then the moment they were through, darted into the hall, and slammed it shut behind her and Lars, who had been huddling behind her legs. Then the two of them set off after the rest of the group, down a side hall whose fluorescent lights flickered on in waves as they moved through it.

Natalie had only visited Tuna Tim's a couple of times as a child; the Prater family were all too aware of Tim's reputation for cutting corners. But from the couple of field trips she'd taken with her school, Natalie remembered what was back here: a cavernous space, all pale blues and silvers like some Olympic pool, but crammed from wall to wall with tiny tanks full of bored-looking fish.

Then she got out of the hallway into the main chamber and realized that the outside of the building wasn't the only thing that had changed.

Yes, there were still tanks, but these were very different. They were huge, like aboveground pools built just high enough for a human adult to lean over. Each one was protected by a wraparound fence with a wide gate, and each fence had a sign with a label FRESHWATER, TIDEWATER, or MARINE MAMMAL.

Adam led them toward the last one. As they approached it, he barked, "Natalie! The keys!"

Natalie raced ahead of them, pulling out the ring of

keys again. This time, she got it right on the second try, opening the gate just in time for the adults, huffing and puffing, to pull Bangor up to the lip.

"Hold on." Adam panted, stopping them before they could slide Bangor into the water. "Natalie, do you see that?"

He jerked his head to the side, and there, leaning against the tank, Natalie saw it—a sort of skeletal raft made of pool noodles, like a floaty stretcher.

Which made sense.

Because Natalie had also just seen the words painted on the far wall.

"What—" she began.

"Natalie," gasped Bob, who was supporting Bangor's back half. "If you wouldn't mind . . ."

"Right. Sorry. Right." Dazed but determined to be helpful, Natalie grabbed the stretcher raft and maneuvered it through the gate and into the water. She held it in place, making sure it didn't float away, while the adults leaned in and finally, slowly, blessedly, lowered Bangor into the tank. The stretcher kept his wound out of the water and kept him floating while he was too weak to swim, but it allowed him, at last, to begin the process of real rehydration.

"Okay," Adam said, rushing to the far side of the room and back again, having grabbed a big blue box with a first aid sign on it and a couple bags of what appeared to be some kind of liquid medicine. "Two of you, hold him still. One on either side, so I can get in the middle. I'm gonna treat the wound first, and then move into inserting the IV."

The more he spoke, the more it all began to make sense. Natalie just kept staring back and forth between him, Bangor, and the words on the wall that read:

OGUNQUIT MARINE LIFE HOSPITAL

As Bob took one side of Bangor's stretcher and Mr. Prater took the other, Natalie's mom noticed her astonishment and stepped closer to her.

"That's what we were trying to tell you, honey," she said. "After the meeting. We found Adam, and he explained everything. He didn't come here to capture animals. He came here to help them."

"But...Aquatic Al's..." Natalie stammered.

But by now, she'd seen enough to predict Adam's next words before he even spoke them.

"Who do you think called the tip in to the press to

shut him down?" Adam said, applying antibiotic ointment to a large cotton swab. "I *hated* working there. I could see right from the first interview that Al was trouble. I would never have taken the job, but, well, marine biology isn't exactly a booming job market. And more important, when I saw those animals in their tiny tanks, I thought, if *I* don't help them... who will? But one person can't fix all the world's wrongs. I was working myself to death, and because I wasn't being my best self, I was letting things slip through the cracks. Which meant animals continued to get mistreated."

He gently began the process of disinfecting Bangor's wound. The porpoise bucked slightly at the sting, and while it hurt to see him hurt, it also made Natalie feel hopeful—that was the most Bangor had moved since they'd found him on the beach. The tank was working.

"So I decided to shut it all down and find somewhere new," Adam continued, not looking up from his work. "Somewhere I could only help, and not hurt. When I heard about your town on the news, I thought, well, *that's* an accident waiting to happen. Which I *was* right about, for the record."

Natalie's dad coughed. Adam looked up and saw some of the goodwill he'd been earning slip away.

"Sorry," he said, almost convincingly. "Polyvinyl bandage, please?"

Natalie decided to put that aside for the moment as Adam moved on to dressing the wound. "Okay," she said. "That's good to know. It's great that you wanted to start a marine hospital here. But why didn't you *tell* anyone this?"

"I didn't trust you all," Adam said, pulling Bangor closer to adhere the bandage to his flank. "I didn't know what kind of connection you had with these animals. I mean, Diver Bob's Sea Life Tours? It was hard to take you all seriously."

"*We* didn't trust *you!*" Natalie retorted. "And Diver Bob is an accredited marine biologist and harbormaster!"

"Well, forgive me for not *thinking* he *acts like one!*"

"No, that's fair, I get that a lot." Bob shrugged.

"Well... I just wish you'd told us," Natalie said. "Because this..." She looked around the room, taking in all the tanks just waiting to heal the animals of the Atlantic. When her eyes settled back on Adam, he was already hooking up the bag of fluids to a drip. "This is impressive," she admitted. "I misjudged you. I'm sorry."

Adam double-checked the IV, inserted it slowly and carefully, and, when he seemed satisfied, turned to face Natalie. Or rather, Natalie's shoes; he didn't seem too eager to look her in the eye just yet.

"Well...maybe you're not the only one who mis-judged," he said. "Without you, Bangor would be in much worse shape than he is now. With how fast we were able to react, and with you looking after him in the truck...because of you, he has a chance at recovery—especially once we finish getting these flu-ids in him. Sure, you went a little overboard when you thought I was a threat to him, but I can relate to going overboard to protect the animals you love."

Now he looked her in the eye. Due to his crouching over to help Bangor, the man and the girl were on equal footing.

"And you really know your animal facts," he said.

"Thank you." Natalie smiled. "I studied."

Just then, voices erupted from the side hallway—the rabble of a crowd drawing closer, and the sound of Mayor Maher yelling, "People, *people*! One at a *time*!"

Nancy Jane poked her head out into the room.

"Folks?" she said. "We can't hold 'em off much longer."

"Where *did* these guys come from?!" Adam huffed, standing up at last.

"Right, so, about that..." Natalie said. "You know how earlier today I thought you were going to ... kidnap a bunch of animals I loved?"

"Yes," Adam said flatly. "I remember."

"Well, back when that was the case ... I may or may not have ... tipped off all those press people who've been hanging around town that they should come to your new place if they wanted a *really* big story."

Adam stared at her, his jaw hanging open. Natalie's dad was doing his usual bad job of trying to look mad when he actually wanted to laugh. Natalie's mom, meanwhile, wasn't even trying to hide the laugh.

"I mean, she was still right," Bob pointed out, trying to get everyone to look on the bright side. "It just wasn't the story she expected!"

It was like the words were a light bulb over Natalie's head.

"Actually ... yeah," she said. "Yeah, he's right. This is a good thing!"

"*How?!*" Adam asked.

"Well, how many employees have you hired for this hospital yet?"

"Zero, but—"

"And how many people did it take for us to get Bangor in here?"

"Four—well, five—well, seven, kind of, or eight counting the dog, *but*—"

"So," Natalie said, grinning, "you go out there, and you meet the press, and you tell them that this is your brand-new marine animal hospital, and it's hiring and open for business! It's free advertising!"

"*Never* turn down free advertising." Bob nodded sagely. "In this media market? Come on."

"But that's..." Adam almost seemed annoyed not to have a better reason to be annoyed. "I was waiting until I was totally sure I was—"

"Mr. Wilson." Now Natalie began to feel like her father—because she couldn't hide her amused smile. "Do you often have trouble reaching out to others for what you need?"

"I..."

Adam's shoulders slumped.

"I've been told that by certain academic advisors, yes," he said.

"I can relate." Natalie grinned. "But I got a chance to change tonight. Here's yours."

Adam looked around at the other adults, waiting for one of them to object. Instead, Mr. Prater smiled proudly at Natalie, and Mrs. Dugnutt and Bob just raised their eyebrows at Adam expectantly.

"Okay," he said at last. "Okay. But somebody needs to stay here and help Bangor."

"I'll do it," said Natalie and Bob at the same time.

"Oh, not *you*," Adam said, gesturing at Natalie. "If I'm setting the story straight that *you* started ... then *you're* helping."

Natalie looked at Bob, who gave her a thumbs-up: *I've got this.*

Well, it only seemed fair. Natalie held out her hand, and after a moment's consideration, Adam reached out and shook it.

Then, the two of them—or three of them, because Lars was right behind Natalie—went to a smiling Nancy Jane, who stepped aside to let loose the media frenzy.

"Hello!" Adam called as the press spilled forth. "And welcome to the Ogunquit Marine Life Hospital. Please, be quiet—we've got a patient receiving care here. I'm Adam Wilson, and I want to tell you all about this first-of-its-kind local institution and how you can help ...

after some *very important* words from my *valued associate,* Natalie Prater."

"I thought her name was Natasha," someone hissed.

"Natalie," said a reporter from Portland News. "It's clear this has been a very eventful night. What's going on here?"

Faced by expectant eyes and ready-to-go recording devices, Natalie took a deep breath.

There would be more to deal with soon, she knew. Like apologizing to some people for her behavior the past few weeks, and somehow making sure the rest of Bangor's pod knew he was okay, and, come to think of it, finding out where Marina had gotten off to—what was *ever* going on in that otter's head?

But Natalie knew that when those challenges came, she wouldn't face them alone.

She reached down.

She scratched a spot behind Lars's ears.

And she smiled.

"Well," she said. "I was hanging out with Lars here tonight, when the strangest thing happened—we were lucky enough to get some help from a friend. Someone you may have heard about, actually. An otter who's been hanging around town..."

CHAPTER NINETEEN
Bangor

Bangor would not miss being out of the ocean.

He would kind of miss flying, though.

Of course, you could have argued that Bangor wasn't precisely "flying" right now so much as "floating in midair," or, even more precisely, "getting carried in a tarp across a cold and windy beach by several straining humans." Still, very few harbor porpoises had gotten to do even that in their lives, so if Bangor wanted to call it flying, who was going to stop him?

It turned out flying was like swimming, but way less work. Uncle York would have loved it.

Human faces bobbed by as Bangor was carried toward the water. It seemed that half of Ogunquit had showed up to watch the flight of the porpoise. Tourists, members of the press, and even a few familiar faces swam past. But all Bangor could focus on right now was the water, glistening ahead of him in the late November light.

The water, and the souls that might—or might not—be waiting for him there.

Bangor's flight came to an end as the humans lowered his tarp to the ground with a symphony of exhausted grunts. The loudest grunt of all came from the human who'd carried the most weight: the one they called Adam Wilson.

Bangor had gotten a lot of chances to study Adam up close over these last few weeks. Up *very* close, actually, considering the amount of time Adam had spent tending to Bangor's wound and monitoring his swimming progress. What Bangor had noticed was that Adam could be curt with other humans, bossing around his handful of new employees and holding them to high standards if they failed to do something just right. But when those humans went away and it was just him and his porpoise patient, well...Bangor saw a whole different side of Adam then. That Adam was attentive, relaxed, and gentle as he helped his patient to heal. When it came to caring for Bangor, Adam Wilson was just that: caring.

Bangor could relate. He knew what it was like to sometimes feel more at ease with members of a different species than your own.

For the thousandth time in the last few weeks, Bangor felt a pang of guilt as he wondered how he was going to find his family—and whether they would even want to see him after what he'd almost done to Bristol.

While he was focusing on this, all the humans he could see were focusing on Adam, expecting the veterinarian to speak, perhaps, about the momentous undertaking they were gathered here to witness. Or maybe he'd thank his new hires for making this possible. Maybe he'd even warmly greet the press.

"I'm not normally one to give big speeches," Adam said.

The crowd held its breath.

"Which is good because we don't have time for them. There's a porpoise waiting. Let's get him in the water."

There was a brief silence, and then laughter, and then full-on cheers. Bangor didn't know what he'd said, but apparently, little by little, Adam Wilson was improving his people skills.

Together with the help of his new staff, all of whom were dressed in wet suits and warm winter hats, Adam bent down, nodded soothingly at Bangor, and lifted him up again, carrying him toward the ocean. Even with Bangor's limited sight line, he could *hear* the water get closer. First there was the sound of the waves lapping at the humans' ankles. Then it was lapping at their hips.

Then it was lapping at Bangor.

Adam didn't miss a beat. The moment he noticed the tarp dipping into the water, he whistled for his crew's attention. With a *slap* of plastic on water, they let the edges of the tarp drop down flat before pulling the whole thing out from under Bangor's belly as swiftly as possible.

The frigid Atlantic rose up to reclaim Bangor as its own.

He had been released.

And not just from captivity. He had been released from pain as well. Where salt water once might have stung against his open wound, now there was just the pleasant smooth rush of water on patched-up skin. Bangor rolled a little from side to side, testing out his new conditions. He floated a small way forward, out from between the marine biologists, curious to see what swimming felt like now, after all these weeks away from the open water.

Within seconds, Bangor knew:

It felt even better than flying.

In a movement so slick and quick it got a gasp from

the crowd on the shore, Bangor shot down into the sea and then right back up to the surface. Puffing for joy, he began to swim in wide, triumphant circles around his helpers, clicking and whistling in exultation.

Then he came to a sudden halt, because all that clicking had picked up something pretty interesting. He pointed his gaze sharply out at the deeper water.

Four eagerly waiting dorsal fins pointed right back at him.

You stayed! Bangor clicked in wild disbelief.

And in a kaleidoscope of cold November sun gleaming off smooth silvery backs, Bangor was reunited with his family.

First to come was Belfast, tearing up the water, unable to contain his energy. Even York was doing happy little rolls through the waves. The boys were back together at last.

Of course, the pod consisted of more than just boys. Bangor peered nervously through a storm cloud of Belfast's bubbles, looking for the family member he both dreaded and wanted to see the most, when a loud voice burst over the water.

"And— Oh, my goodness, folks, this is something really special—it looks like we're just in time to see

Bangor welcomed back by his pod! They seem to be overjoyed to see him!"

Visually, the *Searchin' Urchin* was just a blur on the southern horizon, maintaining a respectful distance from the porpoise family reunion. But a combination of Bangor's excellent hearing and Bob's trademark megaphone allowed him to hear that smiling voice loud and clear:

"Now, you may have heard about this pod, and their friendliest member, Bangor, who's been having a stay at Ogunquit's brand-new aquatic animal hospital. But what you may *not* have known is that those other porpoises in his pod, who are traditionally much shyer, have been seen waiting outside the hospital *every* day for the past two weeks! The mayor of Ogunquit has enacted a slow-traffic zone for this whole area to make sure the porpoises are completely safe while they wait. But how did they know Bangor was inside, you may ask? I'd like to know, too! My theory is that an open window or air vent has allowed them to communicate with Bangor via echolo-cation. It may seem far-fetched, but stranger things have happened—and maybe stranger things did! Part of being a scientist means keeping an open mind to ..."

Bangor may not have spoken human, but the same question had been occurring to him as well.

Wait. He tilted to the side curiously. *How did you all even know where to find me?*

Ask her, Belfast chirped, and rolled to point his snout north along the shore. Bangor followed his indication and saw a brown blur, hanging back in the distance.

Was that . . . Marina? Bangor seemed to have remembered Marina bringing Natalie and Lars to him on the night of his accident, but it seemed so extraordinary and he'd been so woozy at the time that he'd come to wonder if he hadn't made it all up. Could it be she'd done all that—and more?

She's an odd one, Belfast reflected. *A couple weeks ago, Bristol came tearing up to us, squealing her head off about something happening to you in the humans' cove. We all rushed to find you, but when we arrived, you weren't there. She was, though, running up and down the shore like her fur was on fire—and she seemed just about ready to explode if we didn't follow her up the coast here. Seems like she really cares about you.*

Why's she hanging so far back? Bangor asked.

Beats me. For such a pushy otter, she can be kind of shy. Too bad we can't talk to her.

Bangor's thoughts were cut off as York floated right between him and Belfast.

In the meantime, though, York said drolly, *I know someone you can talk to.*

And there, swimming up at last, were Kittery and Bristol. They seemed a little hesitant to approach, and it made Bangor hesitate as well. Even after playing this moment out in his head for weeks on end, he still had no idea how it would go.

Bangor's gaze fell, away from his mother, down toward the ocean floor.

Mom. I'm so sorry. After everything you warned me about . . . I was wrong to act like you were crazy to be scared of humans. I care so much about you, and I don't want to lose you just to have them. If you want, I'll never leave the pod again. I—

Was it the humans who healed you?

Kittery's question stopped Bangor mid-apology.

I . . . yes, he answered. *Yes, it was.*

Then, Kittery clicked, moving closer, *it seems like I'd be lucky to call some of those humans members of my pod. It looks like we were both a little right . . . and both a little wrong. I'm sorry, too.*

And then she had closed the distance between them and was nuzzling her snout against his. And as soon as this had happened, Bristol shot forward and rocketed into Bangor's good side as well, causing the three of them to tumble through the water, laughing and squeaking. And then all five of them were playing together.

"If you're having trouble seeing this amazing sight," Diver Bob boomed, "feel free to look at the zoom lens on the *Searchin'* screen, camerawork courtesy of my lovely first mate, Maria. Now, I know some of you kids wanted to meet the famous Porpoise Girl—my very own incredible stepdaughter, Natalie. But we've been trying to give her some days off recently, so Maria is helping out! And before any of you express disappointment, just know that she's my wife, I love her, and the hiring culture around here is *entirely* corrupt and there's *nothing* you can do about it!"

Now there was one word Bangor recognized: *Natalie.*

Wait, he said, pulling away from the pod to scan the surf. *Where is . . .*

And then a cacophony erupted from behind the dunes on the beach, causing heads to turn.

"Ruff! Wroof, wroof—RUFF!"

"Coming through! Sorry, excuse me! Are we late? Coming through!"

Ah. There they were.

Now Bangor's whole family was *really* reunited.

CHAPTER TWENTY
Lars

"Sorry! In a rush! Sorry!"

"Ruff!"

The dream team was back. Lars knew that he and Natalie were running late, but it didn't matter, so long as they were once again running together. As they crested the last and largest sand dune and hurtled down toward the water, their blind rush was only halted by the sight of Mr. Prater, who stood on the beach with crossed arms and a quiet smile.

"Oh gosh, we completely lost track of time!" Natalie explained, leaning on her knees to catch her breath.

"Ah," Saul Grundy nodded knowingly. "Swim practice? Homework?"

"Nope." Natalie shook her head. "Just hanging with friends."

"Wait for us!"

Keena and KJ came flying over the hill, each

carrying a massive totebag full of every conceivable beach toy or tool.

Natalie smiled at them, and then turned and saw her father's expression.

"Why are you so happy?" she asked.

Mr. Prater bent down to give Lars a scratch, so now they were both happy.

"You may not understand this now," Mr. Prater said, "but it just makes me so glad to see you doing normal kid stuff. And that includes losing track of time with your friends. Trust me, everyone who knows you is happy to wait for you."

Natalie blushed, but for the first time in a long time, it didn't come with the smell of embarrassment or resentment. Instead, Lars picked up the lovely scent of overwhelming gratitude.

"Case in point," Mr. Prater said, gesturing a few yards down the beach. "Bob's not the only one who was happy to help you out today."

"Mister Mayor," said a reporter in a parka, shivering in the November breeze. "Your new initiatives to make Ogunquit a leader in sea life conservation and safety have set off heated debates in town halls all up and down the Maine coast. What advice do you have for—"

"You'll have to pardon me," said Mayor Maher. He was wearing only a thin suit, but he seemed perfectly warm and cozy as if lit by some internal glow. "I'm a little busy right now, actually. I'm helping my fiancée babysit. Isn't that right, Sammy?"

Sammy burst out from between the legs of the mayor and Nancy Jane, speaking loudly for all the viewers back home:

"My name is *Sam*. And I'm not a baby. My *sister's* a baby. And I *wish* she were *here*."

"I thought you didn't like your sister, Sam," Nancy Jane smiled.

Sam shook his head.

"That was the old me," he said. "That was *Sammy*. My friend Natalie gave me a lot to think about over the past few weeks. And she told me that one of the coolest guys I know *loves* having a little sister in his family."

"Oh, yeah? And which guy is that?"

Sam pointed out at the ocean.

"Bangor," Sam said proudly.

Lars and Natalie looked where Sam was pointing, and saw a big porpoise and a little one, floating close together.

"Is he—" Natalie began.

"All healed up." Adam Wilson nodded, appearing beside them, smelling of salt water and pride. "And swimming like a dream."

Natalie smiled. "Perfect."

"Or he *was* swimming," Adam continued, frowning and squinting out at the water. "Now it's like he's... looking for someone?" He looked back and forth between the porpoise and Natalie. "But surely he isn't—"

"Oh, I guarantee you," Mr. Prater said, grinning, "he absolutely is."

That was their cue. Without even a single second glance for the crews and cameras, Lars and Natalie raced for the water. Seeing this, Bangor raced for the shore. In record time, the three of them met in the middle, splashing together in the tall waves, barking and whistling and laughing.

And then three became four, and then more as the rest of the pod pulled up closer. As Kittery approached, Natalie reached out to hold Lars's collar, and Lars tried to doggy paddle as gently as he could.

"Wow." Natalie breathed. "You're *all* coming to say hi, huh? Okay, well, I have a few new folks I'd like to introduce you to as well. They're the best swimmers I know."

Natalie turned and called out:

"Come in slowly! We don't want to come on too strong and scare them—some of them are a little shy!"

"We *never* come on strong!" Keena protested, dropping her beach bag to the ground with a *thud*, as KJ finished strapping on a hot pink snorkel and flippers.

But the girls clearly held a deep respect for Natalie, because they slid smoothly into the water and then executed a gentle breaststroke up to the animals. For a moment, they held completely still, waiting to see what would happen.

Then Bristol zoomed between the twins, which made Keena shriek with surprise, which made KJ point and laugh at Keena, which made Keena splash KJ, which made KJ splash back harder, which meant Lars got splashed—causing him to bark in mock outrage, making both the girls laugh even harder.

And then porpoises, dogs, and girls were all playing together, like the world's biggest, strangest pod, as dozens of humans looked on in amazement.

But it wasn't only humans who were looking on, Lars realized after a few minutes. In all the excitement, he hadn't noticed the smell that was drifting across the water—but some smells were too strong to ignore for long. While the others played around him, he swiveled and saw, in the distance, a pair of big brown eyes poking out of the water.

When Natalie looked up and saw where Lars was looking, the excitement on her face was unmistakable.

"Oh my gosh, you guys! It's Marina! She's here! Hey, c'mere! Come on!"

But the expression in Marina's eyes was, as always, harder to read. She didn't come when Natalie called; she just kept watching Lars and his friends with an expression of...

Curiosity? Hope? Fear? What *was* she ever thinking?

Lars had been wondering this exact question since the night when Marina had found him and led him straight to Bangor. That act of kindness had been the confirmation of everything Lars had started to suspect about Marina: that she wasn't so bad after all, and that she had been trying to connect with Lars this whole time. Even getting stink-bombed didn't seem so bad now, since it was probably the remnants of that otter stink that had allowed Marina to find Lars in the first place.

But even when she was trying to help save Bangor's life, she'd done so skittishly, darting back and forth, practically daring Lars to chase her away for good. What made someone act like that?

Floating there now, making eye contact across the waves, Lars finally saw an answer in Marina's eyes. It was one he was all too familiar with from his many years as a stray. Back then, Lars had never dreamed he'd have a family as big as the one swimming around him now. He'd always assumed it would be either impossible, or so much hassle it wasn't worth it. So he'd pushed people away, keeping the world at paw's length.

Now, though? Now Lars knew how great life could be when you let people get close.

Just like Bangor was getting close to him now, pulling up alongside Lars, supporting him with his comforting bulk while following his friend's gaze out toward Marina.

Bangor sent up a single, inviting:

Puff!

Marina lurched the slightest bit forward—and then stopped again. Those big eyes darted to Lars, clearly wondering if he would snap at her again, if he'd bark like he'd barked before, if he'd push her away for good.

Everyone turned to Lars, waiting to see what he would do next.

What Lars did next was this:

He started to wag his tail so hard that it turned the water around him to foam.

Marina released a small, squeaky gasp.

She quickly groomed her whiskers until she looked her best.

And then she swam toward the biggest, happiest, oddest family Ogunquit had ever seen.

And that family got a little otter.

ACKNOWLEDGMENTS

Every time I get to write a book, I think, *I can't believe they let me write a book!* It's the best feeling in the world. So imagine how I feel about getting to write a sequel. It's the best feeling in the world, multiplied by itself. Heady stuff!

The best feeling in the world is made possible by Orlando Dos Reis, the best editor in the world, based on all available evidence. From helping to plot this book to pushing it across the finish line, he has combined kindness, incisive insight, and deft handling, and in doing so he has made books that are worth reading. He did it with *A Dog's Porpoise* and he's done it again now, not to mention before and in between.

Thanks are due to the rest of the Scholastic team as well. Reading Mary Kate Garmire's copy edits has genuinely become one of my favorite parts of the writing process, and I thank her for that. Thank you, too, to the copyeditor Marcia Santore and proofreader Cailin Evans. Thank you to Angelo Rinaldi for another knockout cover; you clearly just get it. And a supersized sequel's amount of thanks go to David Levithan, who is important for more reasons than just Scholastic-related ones, but who first brought together the dog and the porpoise and me, and who has been unbelievably gracious and patient about responding to questions about every single aspect of the writing process imaginable since then, along with more questions about New Jersey and nineties musical subcultures than he ever signed up for.

Thank you to my family for being my first Maine Research Associates. If you are ever in Bar Harbor, I strongly recommend checking out Diver Ed's Dive-In Theater. It is so fun that you will experience it once and still be writing about it twenty years later, thinking about what a good life your family has given you.

Thank you to Dan Reardon, my interim Maine Research Associate, whose specialty in Ogunquit Studies has now made two books possible, and who now accidentally has a legacy in these books because of it.

Thank you to Bryan, who has risen above and beyond the position of Maine Research Associate to also become something much more important: my writing office landlord. His couch is the best coworking space on the market, and he has proved an inexhaustible investigator of coastal Maine communities, dogs, porpoises, otters, and boats. I believe our work merits further study. I'm very excited.

This book was written across the first half of 2023, and in that time, many people helped just by being around, listening to me talk about otters, or going to Tasty Burger with me at 2 a.m. on my birthday. Those people include but are not limited to: Jack, Paul, Gianina, Jules, Julianna, Danna, Dylan, Mike, Joe, Jo, Z, Arielle, Alex, Grace, Taylor, Conor, Lauren, Colin, and Gal.

As always, thank you to the Q train.

And one more very important thank-you that is required for a sequel: Thank you so much to all the students, teachers, librarians, and readers who passed around *A Dog's Porpoise*, who read it once or twice and told someone about it, and who sometimes even told *me* about it by sending me incredible hand-illustrated letters in the mail. An extra special thank-you to those of you who had to figure out how to read porpoise sounds out loud. I tried to make it easier for you this time around. When all else fails, just have fun with it. That's what I did.

Thanks again.

ABOUT THE AUTHOR

M. C. Ross is an author and playwright living in New York City. His other books include *A Dog's Porpoise, Game Over,* and *Nugly.* He researches his books by spending lots of time in New England and petting lots of dogs. He enjoys his work. For more information, please visit mcrosswrites.com.